LIFE AFTER DEATH

LIFE AFTER DEATH

Brian O'Donnell

NATIONAL
LIBRARY
OF AUSTRALIA

A catalogue record for this book is available from the National Library of Australia

ISBN: 9780648014683-paperback

ISBN: 9780648014690-ebook

Brian O'Donnell

bsodonsm@tpg.com.au

Table of Contents

PREFACE

The top Grammar school in their area had accepted Raymond Clarke into its entry lists for the current year starting in September. Being shy, and self-conscious, Raymond, was a little concerned about his future, but he had always excelled in his academic studies so he ought to be able to compete with his fellow students. Raymond had taken a week's holiday with his boy scout troop on a windswept moor top prior to the big event, when disaster struck.

The local police from Leeds, went looking for Raymond at the campsite because they had some very traumatic news for him. They had the thankless job of telling him that the rest of his family had been wiped out in a road accident, and he was required to travel to Leeds Infirmary with them to identify their bodies. His Grandmother lived on the other side of Leeds, in the village of Clifford, so the police sent a car for her, so they could join up at the hospital and view the bodies together.

The Clarke family were living in a tied cottage, on a large farm, so Raymond would have to remove all their belongings, and move out himself, immediately or sooner. Not yet twelve this task seemed impossible, however with his Granny's help, it had to be done prior to the boy reassembling the mess of his life, and finding somewhere convenient to live and a suitable school to attend. There was some help available from family acquaintances and some smacks in the teeth, that nearly destroyed him, and this 'latter.' at the hands of a rich, so called, "Christian Gentleman Farmer," who should have been in a position to assist him, both with a temporary home, and financial assistance, until he got over the shock and trauma of losing his family, and putting his young life back together. Raymond was ready to move on, but where to? He had successfully passed the eleven plus examinations and was ready for Grammar school, but which Grammar school, and where?

ACKNOWLEDGEMENTS

Actually, writing a book is a very lonely endeavour. It takes for ages and ages whilst shut up in a quiet room, with only my computer, and the office works 'help dog' (windows XP), for company. Only when it's all completed, do I get any real time to look back over the marathon event, and add up all the people who have helped me along the way. Maybe least of all appreciated at the time, is my loving wife, who constantly keeps me satisfied with copious quantities of hot tea, and other goodies, like fresh scones. Sandra has no knowledge or ambitions about computers, and their associated equipment, and would not know a megabyte even if it did actually have the audacity to bite her. I am very fortunate that I have family members who can, and do, support me, especially in a technical way, with their great knowledge of the hardware and programming glitches. David, who as most of you would realise by now, has always been beside me, behind me, and all around me ready to jump in whenever needed, {QUITE OFTEN} and dig me out of the mire. David has forgotten more about computer language, and operating systems, than I am ever likely to learn.

Most important of all are the many anonymous contributors who appear in my daily life, without realising that they are being compromised. It is often the things they say and do, and quite often the things they do not actually say and do, that trigger my imagination, causing it to produce some of the quirky scenarios, with which a story is born. Maybe a warning to all the people I meet and associate with, is a variation of the adage, "Beware you are on candid camera", now reading "Beware you are about to be compromised in a story".

Right at the top of my list are the team members at Pick-A-Woo-Woo Publishing, who diligently sort out my mess and turn it in to a good book. There are one or two of them with the fortitude of a bull dozer, who stick with it through thick and thin. Finally, it gets uploaded to the team at Lightening Source, Ingram Spark who assemble it all together, print it, and bind it into a readable book. My sincere thanks, and appreciation, to all these wonderful people. Well done guys and thank you.

Chapter One

Tragedy and Heartache

Raymond was almost twelve years old and finished with primary school. He had successfully taken, and passed, his eleven plus examinations, with comparative ease, and was ready to tackle grammar school. He went with his parents Elizabeth and John Clarke, to visit the principal at the top grammar school in the area and was accepted as a student for the following year starting early in September. Whilst he was looking forward to the educational challenges to come, Raymond had always been very self-conscious and did not mix freely with his peers. He often felt left out, with a fear of rejection, and often hung back from social participation; due in part to living in a remote farm cottage, with little chance of mixing and communicating with his peers, especially girls; but he had an easy going personality and his school mates were always happy to envelop him in their activities. However, he was never interested in team sports and 'silly' games, as he called them.

He was raised on a remote farm and led a lonely life socially. His old bicycle was his only means of commuting into nearby villages and the local town. His parents had encouraged him to attend, and subsequently join in the local Boy Scouts troop, which suited his personality in spite of a tough three-mile bike ride to get there. There were two very steep hills which he had to walk up because he had no gears on his bike. He enjoyed nature treks and camping, as well as the more formal activities that scouting offered. He was always ready to bear the Standard [flag] during formal activities such as Remembrance Day marches, although when he first attempted the role, he found the flag almost too heavy to carry. None of the other boys were ever interested in the job, so they were happy to leave it to Raymond. The scouts and cubs held a Bob-a-Job week each spring to raise funds, mainly to pay for a week's camping holiday. Both of these activities suited

Raymond's personality, because living on farm, there were always plenty of odd jobs, that the farmers around about, were happy to palm off to a willing youngster, and life in the country on the camps he really enjoyed.

His knowledge and experiences in the woods, fields, and hedgerows, around his home meant that he gained a good deal more from these outdoor treks than the average town kids could, and he was happy to share his experiences and knowledge with the others in his scout troop. Raymond asked his mum if it would be ok for him to go away for a week on the moors with the Scouts during the summer holidays. She said that she reckoned, it would be fine for him to go because he'd done well at the Bob-a-Job work, and the summer camp was part of his reward for a job well done.

However, she said, "Be sure to ask your Dad first, just in case he has other ideas."

The holiday was set to be early in August, including the August Bank Holiday Monday. When he mentioned it to his dad, John said, "Aye, I suppose you might as well since you earned your place, but we intend going to see your

Aunt Edith, and Aunt Grace, so we'll be away all the long weekend. They'll be disappointed if you don't go, but as you have never, ever met either of them, I don't suppose it will matter much. After all they've never bothered to come and visit your mum, and she acted as mother to them both for many years after your Granny Howarth died, and they were still very little. Aye, alright then away you go but keep out of trouble. Hang on a minute, you'll need a bit of spending money in your pocket, so here you are son." He fished out his wallet, extracted a pound note and handed it to his son. Raymond was amazed at this show of generosity, after all a pound was quite a lot of money in those days, and he said, "Gee thanks dad, this will make my trip much more fun. I hope you all have a lovely trip. It's a long way to go, isn't it? Don't they live the other side of Coventry?"

"Aye you're right about that. I reckon it's about 140 miles each way, but the old Standard will get us there and back in great shape. She's not the fastest car on the road, but very reliable."

The few days before the weekend were a bit hectic as they all collected and packed their expected needs for their trips. Raymond had a scout's kit bag into which he packed all his gear, and his toiletries went into a side pocket for easy access. He would have to wear his uniform for the trip of course, and he was ready. John agreed to deliver him, and his kit to the assembly point, telling him he would meet him there the following weekend to bring him home.

As they approached the rendezvous point a brand-new looking lorry passed them travelling in the opposite direction and Raymond excitedly called out, "Hey Dad, look, that's one of them new type of lorries that were in the paper last week. They have a weird sort of diesel engine. It's a two stroke not a four stroke and the cylinders are horizontal not vertical. Because the engine is flat, the cabin sits on top of it and right up at the front. They have air brakes too, which are so powerful that they have to have warning signs on the rear end, to stop following traffic smashing into the back of them."

"Aye, all that's right enough, but they really need them brakes, because the two-stroke engine doesn't hold them back on the hills, like a normal engine. My old pal Bobby drives one of them for his boss, and he hates them in hilly country. They are powerful and climb like the devil but they are dynamite on the steeper downhill runs, he has to be extra careful when he goes over a crest until he gets the feel of the gradient, before he starts to run downhill. He had a couple of scary moments until he worked out the correct procedure before starting the decent. Now he leaves the gearbox in low gear over the crest, until he gets the feel of the gradient. He reckons it's a lot easier to change up a gear or two if suitable, but never down a gear at all."

Around eight o'clock, a furniture truck pulled into the yard in front of the hall, and all the boys were instructed to load in their kitbags and climb in after them. Raymond arranged his kit bag with the side pocket sideways so as not to squash the toothpaste etc. then sat comfortably on the top of the bag for the journey. According to the lorry driver, they were headed to a campsite on Brampton moor near the town of Ostlay, so they were to travel about thirty miles and due to all the hills in between, it would be a slow trip for the ancient Bedford. The area around the camp site was known as Brampton moor but did not include the village of Brampton itself. There was a very steep climb beyond the village, high up onto the top of the moor. The scenery was stunningly beautiful and seemingly endless with miles of heather in full flower and plenty of bright yellow gorse bushes.

After a long, slow crawl up onto the moor top, they eventually entered a gateway in the dry-stone wall. There was a large wooden hall ahead of them and what looked like an ablution block at one end. They hadn't sighted any homesteads or other buildings along the way, as they climbed up out of Wharfedale onto the moor tops.

Raymond soon realized, that the one-pound note in his purse would almost certainly stay there, because, there was absolutely nowhere within miles to spend any of it. Up there on the moor, there was only the moor and mother nature, along with her friends, the birds, bees, and wild animals and unending stretches of virgin heather. Occasionally there were outcrops of rocks, surrounded by thickets of bright yellow gorse bushes in full flower.

Once the boys had unloaded their kitbags, and selected a place against the side wall of the hut, they were told to go around to the ablution block to freshen up before lunch. After the first shock of finding themselves at sea, in a never-ending moorland, there came another. There was a single row of taps above a long wash trough, but only icy cold spring water, gushed from any one of them. There was plenty of it but it was all icy cold. There were no facilities at Brampton to heat the water for washing or bathing. Large kettles were supplied in the main hut, to brew hot drinks and wash pots and crockery. There was a large gas stove to heat the kettles and cooking pots, but nothing to wash sweaty bodies. The lack of hot water was no imposition to Raymond, however, because there was no hot water system in his previous home, only one cold-water tap over the kitchen sink. He was used to washing himself in the small streams that abounded the area where he lived. As he travelled around the countryside he often swilled his face and hands and upper body in a convenient stream, and on sunny days, he regularly went skinny dipping, in a small secret pool on the sweeping bend in the beck, [large stream] about a mile away from home. At least up here at the camp he had towels to dry himself whereas at home, near the beck, he could only wipe the excess water off his various body parts using the palms of his hands, and leave the rest to dry off in the wind, and sometimes the sun, if he was lucky.

Lunch consisted of a selection of sandwiches, which the Scout leaders had brought with them from town. After lunch, Raymond and his friends, Paul and Adrian, were delegated to find enough tinder and kindling to start a cooking fire outside, in the designated area surrounded with stones, then split some logs to keep the fire going, ready to cook large pots of stew on the coals for their evening meal. Other boys were delegated to prepare vegetables to add to the juicy soup bones, and off cuts of meat, donated by a local butcher back home. When the chores had been attended to everyone pitched in for a friendly game of football. True to his nature though, Raymond and his two friends, Paul and Adrian, who like him were nature lovers, went for a good long walk through the heather, down the steep side of the moor to where there was a small stream, running and gurgling along the stony bottom, and through some stunted trees and bushes. They soon discovered that this area was vastly different to the area where they all lived. The bushes and trees were quite different, not just stunted but different species, and the birds were also different, although there were a few familiar faces amongst them. There were swallows and swifts, and naturally the odd crow or two. There was a strange curling sound coming intermittently from the moor around where they were walking, which Raymond identified as a curlew. All this was good because, as part of scouting, they were expected to keep a log of natural things that they had observed along the way and this was a great start for the week.

As they were walking along the stream, Raymond suddenly stopped and placed his fingers on his mouth to signal the others to silence. He pointed to a thick clump of vegetation and held his breath until his pals got the message. Their eyes were not as attuned to wildlife as Raymond's were but gradually one of them, then the other picked out a pair of eyes in the bushes. They whispered what sort of animal is that. The animal, suddenly turned around and disappeared, through into the thicker cover. Raymond said, "That was almost certainly a fox and I am sure it was only a young cub. We would never have got as close as that to an adult fox in daylight. We're so lucky we came out for a ramble on the moor instead of playing football. All we need to do now is log all our sightings in our diaries and Red six is well on the way to being top dog for the week. Just keep this location secret so as not to help the others. If we get chance later in the week, how about we spend a bit of time down here because their den must be nearby and we may get to see the others as well."

Paul replied, "Wow, I'm glad we came with you, Ray. It will be a tough week if we're to get maximum points for our nature and wildlife badges, but this is a good start. Come on you two we must get back quickly or we'll lose points for being late." A brisk trot back up the hillside got them onto the playing area whilst the others were still kicking the ball around. They went inside the hut to get their pencils and diaries to record all the afternoon's events whilst they were still fresh in their minds, before heading round to the ablution block for toileting and a good wash up of hands and faces ready for tea.

Back in the camp the large pot of stew was almost perfectly cooked, so they began slicing the big crusty loaves and arranging the soup dishes ready for dinner. Having already washed their hands ahead of the mob they were ready to dish up the meal. The senior scout leaders joined them to organize the meal as the other boys began to join in. Once everyone was gathered around, the leader called for the reciting of the Scout's Law, and Scout's promise, followed by the singing of the national anthem, before a senior scout said grace, then it was a free for all to get a good feed. After clearing away the remains of their dinner and washing the crockery. They were asked to prepare dishes and plates ready for breakfast, then they had free time until lights out. One of the senior scouts had brought along his old squeeze box, and soon everyone was singing their hearts out to the stains of the old campfire songs. Foam bedrolls had been provided to ease the discomfort of the wooden boards and a mob of very tired lads were soon asleep. Most slept well until they were awakened by an unearthly racket. Someone, who still needed a lot of tuition and practice, was blasting away on a bugle. Bad though it was it had the desired effect. Soon all the boys were up and about, hoping for a big breakfast. This was likely to occur but only later.

Once everyone was out of bed on this Sunday morning, and swilled their faces in the trough they were called to assembly. The scout law and promise were recited, then the senior scout with the squeeze box began to play a poplar hymn tune. Soon all the group were singing their favourite hymns, before repeating the Lord's Prayer. The Sermon was only a short speech rendered by the head scout, and it was followed by the National Anthem.

Breakfast consisted of piles of toast with a heap of scrambled eggs and baked beans. Most of the toast was grilled on the rekindled fire, but some had to be cooked in the kitchen, to keep everyone satisfied. The kettles were boiling, and tea or cocoa was freely dispensed for all. After eating, the pots and pans were quickly dealt with then, they all took turns in preparing vegetables ready for lunch. Those not actually peeling and cutting up spuds and carrots were busy kicking a football around, and one small group were measuring out the playing field ready for a game of cricket during the afternoon. There were a couple of extra players because four sixers make 24 not 22 so Paul and Raymond elected to go rambling again. Adrian was sent out onto the far boundary to field and from there it was easy to 'get lost' and disappear to join the rambling group. Hopefully he would not be missed, at least until his side had to bat. This time all three of the boys had brought their note books and pencils, to record any sightings as they went. They took a roundabout route down to the stream, then doubled back to the place where they had seen the fox cub. They recorded sightings of dragon flies, butterflies some assorted birds and many wild flowers, avoiding the gorse bushes, of course, and trying not to awaken the dead with their noise, and soon they were in a small clearing. Beyond, there was a fair-sized clump of rocks which they carefully circled, and lay down on a flat area of rock on the other side. The breeze was in their faces as they watched the cleared area beyond the rocks. After a little while when they were almost dropping off to sleep one fox cub warily appeared and it was soon followed by three more. The cubs began to roll around and play together in the sun. Snarling, growling and biting one another in play. They had so much energy, and they raced around and around the clearing. Ray was soon ready to move on so he circled out behind the rocks and continued up the stream. Once they were clear of the foxes, they sat on another rocky outcrop to write up their notes. The rocks were quite warm after bathing in the sun, so the boys stretched out as comfortable as possible and promptly fell asleep.

It was Paul who woke up first and he jumped up in a panic shouting, "Come on you two wake up quick. It's really late, almost dark in fact. We'll be in terrible trouble. Everyone will be out looking for us, come on, hurry up you two."

Ray calmed Paul down then replied, "We aren't late but we need to get back. Look at the sky, it's come over very cloudy and black. It looks like it'll rain any time now, maybe even a thunder storm, and lightening."

They headed back down the stream which was mostly encased in high banks making it seem even darker. They were about back to where they came down the moor slope, when Adrian yelled out as something zoomed past his face. He said, "What the heck was that, it nearly got me. It must have been some sort of a bird but it had very long wings. Come on you two let's get out of here quickly before it attacks us."

Raymond and Paul were enjoying a good old laugh at poor Adrian, the dedicated townie, who was flapping his hands around his head, trying to keep the weird animal, or what-ever it was, away from his face.

"No silly, it was only a little old bat." Ray told him.

"Oh my god, your saying there are bats around here. You mean those black things with long wings and a mouth full of needle-sharp teeth. They bite your neck when you're asleep and suck out your blood until you're dead, don't they?"

"Silly old Adrian, you read too many comics. Bats come in many different types and sizes, some smaller than a mouse and some as big as a cat. In tropical areas they have fruit bats which are huge, probably around ten or even twelve pounds apiece but they only feed on ripe fruit. I didn't get much of a look at that one, but it was probably only a short-eared bat or something like that. They are harmless if you leave them alone. But they will bite your finger if you grab hold of them. Come on let's get back to camp quickly before the storm breaks."

When they neared the camp-site they could see that the cricket match was just finishing, and the others were collecting up the equipment quickly ahead of the storm, so they joined up with the fielding team and hurried in together to the booming and crashing of thunder, and great flashes of lightening.

Surprisingly, there was a police car coming in through the gateway off the road and it stopped near the huts. A police Sergeant jumped out of the passenger side door and hurried over to the fireplace where everyone was assembling. He asked the Scout Leader, "Have you a scout here called Raymond Clarke, pal?"

The leader replied "Yes, he's here somewhere, but I'm not sure where. They're just coming in now, look. Why are you looking for Raymond? Is he in some sort of trouble?"

"Have you got somewhere a bit more private where we can go for a chat?"

"Yes, come with me into the caretaker's office and we can send Raymond in to you. Oh, there he is now, the middle one of those three scouts." When Raymond walked into the office the Sergeant said, "Come in, and sit down, pal, we have some bad news for you, really bad news. Do you know where the rest of your family is at the moment?"

"Not really sir, only roughly that is. They went to see my aunties near Coventry for the weekend, and they should be back home by about 8 o'clock tonight, if the old car went well. Why are you here? Has something gone wrong with the car?" Asked Raymond.

"I'm afraid it's a lot worse than that Raymond. They were coming home as you said, but a runaway lorry, came down a side road and smashed into them. The road there is all walled in with stone blocks, so they were smashed through the wall and into the field beyond. The lorry was loaded, and the brakes failed completely. There's not much left of the car, it was flattened against the wall, and most of the load landed on top of it. We are sure it was your people because of the documents in their possession, and we were able to read the rear number plate. I am sorry to have to tell you, this but they were all killed instantly, but one good thing is they would not have suffered at all.

In the front, there was your father, one John Clarke, according to his license, who was driving and your mother Enid Jenifer Clarke beside him. There was a young teenage girl in the rear seat who we believe may be your sister, Georgina Clarke. I understand the trauma of all this heaped on you but we need to have someone identify the bodies as soon as we can arrange it. Is there someone, a relation nearby who could be there with you at the hospital in Leeds."

"My Grandmother lives at the other side of Leeds in Clifford village, but she has a bad leg, a club foot in fact, and would need to be collected and driven there. She has to use a walking stick to get around at all. Anyway; there's no way she could get there tonight. There'll be no buses at this time today."

"That's ok. I'll send a car for her, if you have the address, and if you would be good enough to collect your belongings, we can set off straight away and meet her at the hospital. You most likely won't be coming back here at all, I'm really so sorry about that young man."

"I have Grandma's address in my pack so I'll get that and pack up my kit. Sergeant, are you sure that all my family are actually dead? It's not some big mistake is it. Without my Dad I will have to find somewhere else to live and put all our furniture and gear. We live in a tied cottage you see, and Dad's boss is as mean as sin. He'll kick me out quick smart so he can use the cottage for his next tractor driver, if he can find someone who'll work for him."

"You have no need to worry about all that just yet, Raymond, and the police department will assist as much as they can. Come on now, if you have all your kit let's get cracking."

"Sergeant, can you tell me how the accident actually happened?" Asked Raymond.

"We only have a preliminary report as yet and it is pretty damning against the manufacturers of the lorry. Those new lorries have a full air braking system They rely on air pressure to apply the brakes. If the air pressure drops, they have no brakes what-so-ever. It only takes a burst or cracked pipe to allow the air to leak out. They have no mechanical connection between the drivers pedal and the actual brake bands, so no air pressure, no brakes what-so-ever, not even a handbrake. The ministry of transport has issued a recall notice and every one of them has to be returned to the dealerships to have the whole system replaced. They have been lucky until to today, because there have been no accidents due to the brakes failing. This is the first one to cause a smash, let alone any fatalities. Most of the lorries have already been modified, and this was to be the last trip for this one before going in to be altered next week. The owner will be in trouble too, because he was ordered to pull this one off the road before the deadline; Friday of last week."

Raymond said, "Oh heck, I was supposed to go with the rest of the family, to visit our relations this weekend, and it was only because of this camp that I wasn't with them, and possibly killed as well."

He was trying desperately to keep his composure as he thanked the scout leader, and bade farewell to all his mates. They were all wondering what had happened to cause the visit from the police, and his early departure, especially Paul and Adrian. The scout leaders called everyone together and just told them that his parents had been in a very serious accident, in their car, but neglected to tell them of the fatal outcome He climbed into the rear seat of the police car and the sergeant got in beside him. Once they were on the move, the sergeant who was a family man himself, placed his arm around him and pulled him close then extended the other arm and gripped Raymond's left hand and gave it a little squeeze. That action opened the flood gates, as Raymond settled into his embrace and poured his little heart out. He cried and sobbed all the way to the outskirts of Leeds city and the sergeant comforted him and encouraged him to let it all out. Once he settled down a little, he looked around to see where they were, although he had very little experience of most of the city. Dodging trams and pedestrians the constable drove into the hospital car park. Raymond asked the sergeant, "How did you know where to find me Sergeant."

"Once we had your dad's address from his wallet, we sent a local Bobby to the cottage. There the lady next door, told him that you had gone to a scout camp on the moors somewhere near Ostlay. The local policeman telephoned head office in Leeds and I was sent out to try and find you. I live in Harewood village you see, and I know this area very well, and there was only one place that I knew of that fitted the bill."

Raymond was somewhere between being terrified, and just plain numb, as the sergeant assisted him to stand up and walk to the door. Another police car was parked nearby and a little old lady stepped out, and was handed her walking stick, and Raymond realized it was his Granny. He left the policeman behind and ran over to greet and hug his Grandmother. They were both crying their hearts out and consoling each other as best they could. The sergeant stood back, until the pair were more settled, then escorted them inside the hospital. A nursing sister met them in the entrance hall with a wheel chair for his Granny, introduced herself, and escorted them to the mortuary. The hospital staff were ready for them and led them inside the viewing room. An attendant pulled out a refrigerated drawer with a body on the trolley covered with a sheet. A Doctor stepped forward saying, "Please, do either of you recognize this gentleman? Just take your time there is no hurry."

Raymond stepped forward ahead of his Granny took a quick look before declaring in horror, "That's my Dad alright. His name's John Clarke."

His Granny moved in beside him and said, "Aye that's right love, that's your Dad alright, John Clarke. He lived and worked on a farm near Granby"

They both stood back away from the trolley, which the attendant replaced and pulled out the next one. He uncovered the slightly battered face of the lady. The left side of her face was badly damaged where she had hit the side window of the car, but Raymond was in no doubt who the lady was saying, "And that's my Mum. Her name is Enid Jennifer Clarke."

Again, his Granny stepped forward and said, "Oh my God, you are right lad, that's your Mother right enough." They shared a long cuddle and a heap of tears whilst the attendant covered the body again.

They both moved back again as the attendant wheeled the trolley back into place, and wheeled out the next one, and uncovered the bruised face of a teenage girl. "Look Gran this is our Georgina, Georgina Clarke, she's my older sister, she's only seventeen."

Again, his Gran confirmed the identity of the corpse. They were both left speechless, but Raymond rallied enough to give his Granny a huge hug, before staggering out through the door, back into the corridor with her, and out of that horrible room, holding onto her arm. The attendant nurse retrieved the wheel chair, and helped to wheel his Grandmother out and down to the reception area. The staff organized a cup of tea each for them as Raymond asked, "What are we going to do now Gran? Here comes the police sergeant again. Can you manage a night at our place so I can feed the pigs, then we'll have to start sorting things out between us? I hope the police can take me home because it'll be awkward; in fact, totally impossible tonight; and difficult even tomorrow, by bus from here, this late in the day. Being as it's a holiday Monday, doesn't help either. In fact, I think it will be impossible to go by bus until morning, or even the next day, and it'll be difficult even then. Even on a normal day there are no buses this late in the day, and we would need to change buses at Harrogate and Hendon Bridge. Maybe we could get a bus to your place, but I need my bike and the pigs will be starving hungry. I just have to get home tonight if possible, to prepare food for our pigs. I'll have to slice up a bucket full of sugar beet and cook it overnight so I can feed them first thing in the morning."

Chapter Two

Home To An Empty House

The police sergeant, came over and asked them if they had decided where to go next, and how could he help. Raymond ran through the options, and he said that his Granny could get back home from the farm by United Bus into York city, any time in the next few days, and that would give them time to start organizing funeral services etc. He said, "Please can you organize a car to take us to my home near Granby, because there'll not be any buses now until tomorrow morning, and our pigs will be starving hungry by now."

The sergeant rang his superiors and was granted permission to take them home to the farm. Raymond helped his Gran into the rear seat and he climbed into the front seat next to the driver so that he could navigate. He told the driver to go via Harrogate and

Knaresborough. Amazingly both he and his Gran were sound asleep before they cleared Leeds streets. When he woke up they were negotiating driving through the bottom end of Knaresborough town, so he sat up and guided them out into the country, across the Great North road, and the York road, before running through a network of country lanes, and finally along a cart track near the river Ouse, and to the cottage that Raymond pointed out. He had taken a front door latch key to the camp so they were able to get in without any bother. It was very late when he thanked the sergeant, and stepped into the cold, empty, house. The Sergeant asked if they could manage now or was there something that he could help with. He, the Sergeant, stepped back into the car, commenting to the driver, "I hope you can find your way back from here, because I couldn't."

Entering the house fair gave Raymond the shivers, so he held onto his Granny and shared some comfort and cuddles. Raymond lit the kerosene primus stove and put the kettle on for a quick cup of tea and cocoa. He had to light the kerosene primus stove to get some boiling water, because there was no electricity in the cottage, but that only took a few minutes. There was no fresh milk but there was a tin of condensed milk in the pantry, which sufficed their needs for now.

Both Raymond and his Gran were about very early next morning. Raymond brought in kindling, and fire wood, and soon had a good fire going. The fire was necessary to heat up the water system because this house, unlike their previous dwelling had a built-in hot water system, and he was desperate for a hot bath to soak away his aches and pains. Also, he had to boil up some sugar beet to feed the pigs. He set the kettle on to boil then jumped on his bike for a quick trip to a neighbouring farm to collect a billycan full of fresh milk, and a dozen eggs for breakfast. There was part of a leg of ham hanging in the pantry as usual so he cut a few slices off it to go with the fried eggs. They had to manage without bread until he could get to town for some shopping or maybe his Gran could bake a loaf or two whilst he was away. Raymond collected a note book and biro before sitting down for breakfast. As they ate, he and Gran discussed plans for the future. They made a comprehensive list of to-dos. He had called in to see the cowman's wife down the road near the other farm and explained what had happened to his family, then dropped in next door to the horseman's home to let them know what was happening. They were all stunned to hear the news and full of sympathy, promising to help as much as possible. As soon as they had a good fire going, Raymond sliced a bucket full of sugar beet by hand, to be boiled up for the poor old pigs. He knew they would be ravenously hungry so he mixed up a feed of barley meal and water to keep them going, and took it down to feed them for now, then as soon as the food was cooked, he headed off to the pig yard again where he was mobbed by the still hungry animals. As he walked back to the cottage, he realized that sorting out the pigs would have to be top priority. There was only enough barley meal for few days left in the shed, so they would need to be gone by the weekend or early next week at the latest. There was still a reasonable pile of sugar beet but they needed the barley meal as well.

Raymond's Granny had been a midwife most of her adult life in spite of her club foot, and she was very fastidious about cleanliness and tidiness, so he left her at the cottage to begin packing up their belongings, and scrubbing the place out for one last time. Raymond told her not to be too particular because the farmer would kick them out quick smart, as soon as he knew what had happened, but his Gran retorted that the place would be left immaculate. No one would be able to point the finger at them for leaving it mucky.

Raymond hopped aboard his trusty old bike and headed for a nearby town. On the outskirts of town there was the biggest farm live stock trading venue in the county. It was run by a dynamic family of auctioneers, three generations of them in fact. They were all very capable auctioneers and very well thought of as model citizens, as well as business people. The Anderson Family were very helpful and caring people so Raymond felt he would be able to trust them to help sort out the pig problem. Due to a delay after the Bank holiday it was sale time at Korby Bend, so he went straight to the sale yards. As soon as he was able, he went over to have a quick chat with one of the younger members, who mainly dealt with the pigs. James was able to spare him a few moments between yards, so, Raymond quickly explained his problems. The family who were well known to the Clarke family were deeply shocked to hear of the tragedy and vowed to help wherever they could. Raymond explained about the pigs and asking if he could put them up for sale next Monday. James said that would be fine but how would he bring them in. Raymond said that his dad always used a backyard carrier from a nearby village who uses a horse and cart so he would have to talk to him to see if he was willing to handle them and if he would have time available. James asked, when would he like to move the pigs. Raymond said that because of the problems with the farmer, he wanted to load them on Sunday morning, whilst the boss was at church, to avoid a major row, but it would depend if the horse and cart were available.

James was tickled pink by all this devious-ness as he had no liking for this mean, tight fisted, and difficult farmer. He came back at Raymond with a better solution. He said, "Can we get a horse box in there behind my Land-Rover? Will they be hard to load on to a trailer?"

Raymond said, "There's a public right-of-way running alongside the pig yard from road to road and the pigs are really pets. I'll make sure they are very hungry and they'll load themselves."

"You seem to know all the tricks of the trade, so tell me how to get there, and we'll see you about 10.30am on Sunday morning." Raymond was delighted and drew little map to show the way in. James asked Raymond, "What are you going to do about arrangements for a family funeral. Have you been able to make any arrangements yet?

"No; the accident only happened last night and I only have my Granny to help me. There is no telephone at the cottage and Mr, Fernleigh will be too miserable to let me use the farm phone. I was hoping to see what I can do whilst I am in town this morning. I have no idea where to begin. I'll need an undertaker, coffins, and goodness knows what else. On top of all that Mr. Fernleigh will chuck me out of house immediately, because he'll need to hire another tractor driver, who'll move into our cottage."

"Ok, young man, you need to set a number of processes in motion. I have to get back to the sale for now, but if you go into our office in town and ask for Janine Brody, and she'll attend to most of your problems. Do you know where the office is situated in town, Raymond?"

"Yes Sir, it's alongside the bank building in the town square, isn't it?

"That's correct pal. You get along there now and I'll ring Janine and tell her to expect you."

"Gosh Mr. Anderson that'll be a great help and thank you for sorting out my pigs as well."

As promised Janine was well versed in all legal issues and soon had the ball rolling. Firstly, she asked if he had any thoughts about a suitable burial site, and maybe a funeral director. Raymond said he thought the best place to inter his family was in the Catholic grave yard in Clifford village, alongside his grandfather, because that was quite close to the infirmary. The Catholic Church people knew the family well, so he said it would be best there, then they would all be together. Janine consulted the phone directory and was soon discussing the funeral details with Father O'Malley. He said he would arrange a local funeral firm to collect the bodies, transfer them to Bramham initially, and supply the necessary coffins and other necessities. Janine insisted in getting the details of the undertaker, so she could telephone him to make sure that he did the best for Raymond's family, at a fair and reasonable price, because Raymond had no money, nor did he have sure access to any at that point of time. The church officials, and Mother Superior at the convent came onboard to help with temporary funds to cover expenses.

Raymond remembered the regular payments his mother had made to the prudential insurance company every month, so Janine rang the Leeds office, and discovered that both Raymond's Mother and Father were well insured against sudden, accidental death, so there would be enough money for the funerals and plenty to get his own life organized. When

James Anderson returned to the office, he joined Janine and Raymond with a mug of tea, then sat down with them both for a chat. He asked Raymond, "Can you tell us what happened to your family. Do you have any details that might help?"

Raymond replied, "Only the little that the police sergeant told me on the way to the infirmary. He reckoned there would be a big stink before it was all sorted out. He said the lorry was faulty even though it was quite new. The maker would be in big trouble for issuing a faulty vehicle but the local dealer, and the owner would get into trouble too, because the lorry was not supposed to be on the roads after last Friday. The factory had issued an urgent recall to change the faulty braking system before it could be driven on the roads again". Janine had written all that down and vowed to deal with it. She realised that, given time, there should eventually be a substantial compensation package for Raymond. Raymond was able to name the make and model of the lorry and the police had given him the registration details. They also gave him the details of the local dealership, purported to have sold the lorry, and failed to pull it off the road as ordered by the Ministry of Transport. James asked Janine to contact all the relevant people and attempt, in fact demand, that sufficient funds were to be made available immediately, to cover the funeral costs, and rehousing of Raymond, to help him put his life back in order.

Raymond rode back home to reassure his worried Grandma. He had been gone a long while and she had spent the day drinking tea and smoking cigarettes with the two farm workers wives. As expected, she had baked a couple of loaves of bread and some teacakes. By the time Ray arrived back home, she also had a batch of scones cooling on a wire tray

It happened late, on the day following their return to the cottage, to get things sorted, that the farmer walked down to the cottage to have a chat with Raymond. He asked him about his pigs and disposal of the same. Raymond was astute enough not to mention his visit to the auctioneer and the arrangements that had taken place on the Sunday morning. He only told him that he was hoping to sell them to help with their immediate funds, because he was desperately short of cash until the insurance and any compensation was available, so the farmer offered to take them off his hands. He said, "Now look here boy, as you know they aren't worth much because they need a lot more feeding to be marketable, so I'll give you a fiver for them and take them off your hands so you need have no more worries in that direction. Raymond was stunned and replied, "Do you mean a fiver for the two pigs. They are worth a lot more than that because they are almost ready for bacon. This is thanks to my Dad for fourteen years of toiling and caring for your business. Only Dad could repair your machinery and keep it running. If you'd had to call in the local blacksmith, or the engineer from Hunsingore, every time one of your machines broke down it would have cost you a fortune, not to mention the down time at critical periods of the seasons."

"That's alright for you but they'll have to be gone by the weekend. If they are still in my orchard or anywhere else on my farm next Monday morning, I'll lock the gates and impound them. They will be mine. So, you had better think again my lad. I tell you what, I'll double my offer to five pounds each. I have the cash here now so what do you reckon."

Raymond held his ground and demanded a lot more money before he would sell the pigs.

"Aye, that's what I thought you'd say. Your just as stubborn as your old man. You'll regret this day's doings." Replied the farmer, Mr.Fernleigh, before storming off, back home.

Raymond brewed up a pot of tea and toasted some bread for their supper. As they were enjoying their supper Granny asked, "Why didn't you tell Fernleigh that you have already sold the pigs and had arranged their removal from his farm, love?"

"Well the answer is simple Gran, he never asked me, did he? Anyway, he would have found some way to stop the removal. He wants my pigs but is too mean to pay a fair price for them."

"All the same love it would have been good to get the mean old sod off your back and leave you in peace."

"Gran, do you actually expect him to leave us in peace? Like heck he will, he'll be here again early every morning to hassle us to finish packing and get out of here, never mind about the pigs they're the least of our worries."

On the next Sunday morning, Raymond took another bucket of fresh pig food down to the orchard, and as soon as the boss drove out with his family. He signalled James to pull his Land-rover and horse trailer alongside the yard. They helped Raymond to carry the heavy steel trough into the horse box and sit it against the front wall. He opened the gate and slowly tipped the still, warm mash into the trough. They were nearly knocked over in the rush as the hungry pigs ran up the ramp and began to gobble their food. Well boys I hope you noticed that cunning little trick. It might come in handy one day. The box was fitted with side gates across the back of the trailer which the boys quickly closed before lifting up the tail ramp. James was about to do a 'u' turn until Raymond stopped him and told him to go straight forward out onto the other road. There were only two gates in the way which the boys opened and closed behind them. That was it: job well done.

Raymond returned back to the cottage to assist his Granny pack his belongings, but he had no idea where to, or how, he was going to get all the family possessions to wherever that might be. He thought he should telephone the auctioneer to arrange a suitable lorry, to move all his stuff, but first he needed to find somewhere to store everything, until he found somewhere to live. Temporarily he could live in the spare bedroom at his Granny's council unit once all their possessions were sorted.

Raymond cycled to the nearby village of Granby the next day to telephone the auctioneers and was told that the sale had been well attended and top price obtained for his pigs. James said they brought 32pounds ten shillings each and Raymond could collect the cash any time he was in town. Raymond asked James how much the net price would actually be and James retorted, "Can't you add up Raymond, twice times 32pound ten, is 65 pounds. All the costs have been absorbed as our gift to help you out, and thank you for the business and a lesson or two. for my boys. Good luck for your future, and don't hesitate to give us a call if you need any help, at any time in the future." Raymond was overwhelmed with gratitude and thanked him profusely.

When he arrived back at the cottage Granny was amazed and delighted, giving him a great big hug and kiss. Granny caught a United bus later in the day and headed off home, leaving Raymond to continue the sorting and packing their belongings. All the family's clothes he packed into a couple of large boxes to be delivered to the Salvation Army. Clever old Granny Clarke suddenly remembered an old friend of his Grandad, who lived in a nearby town close to where she lived. He ran a business as a second-hand furniture dealer in the main street. She hopped off the bus in Tadminster main street, which left her only a short walk to the second-hand furniture shop. Granny was welcomed by the shop keeper and given a chair to sit on whilst she told her sorry tale. He called his wife, from the living quarters at the rear of the shop, to console and comfort Gran with a cup of sweet tea, then picked up his appointment book to see when he could get to the farm. He promised to drive over to the farm early on the following, Tuesday, morning to see what he could do. Ray planned to be gone from there by the following Monday or Tuesday after the removal of his pigs, if they could organize a lorry to take their belongings away. The lorry actually arrived on Monday afternoon, bringing Granny with him, and a couple of handy lads as well. They soon had a full load of the bigger furniture in his removal van, and left them with a heap of packing cartons and boxes for all the odds and ends. They were able to clear out everything from upstairs so that Granny could attack it with her cleaning kit. The lady from next door and the cowman's wife turned up to help out and soon everything was packed into boxes except for a few clothes and essential kitchen items that they would need. The four of them got stuck into the upper floor together, and by the time they were ready for bed, all was spick and span. Just another good load in the morning when the lorry returned, and they would be on their way. and good riddance to this mean, cranky, old farmer.

The next morning, Tuesday, they both rose early to finish the packing and wait for the lorry to return. By the time the men arrived mid-afternoon, most of the cleaning had already been completed. The lorry was reversed close to the front door and duly loaded with the rest of Raymond's worldly goods. Mr. Fernleigh, the farmer walked down mid-way through the loading and was obviously in a foul mood. He yelled at Raymond, saying "What the hell are you lot doing here still, you were supposed to be gone by last Friday? I need your house so I can employ another tractor driver, since your Dad has left me in a hole, and we have to get started with the harvest. We need the tractor to pull the binder. Unknown to him at that time, he would still be trying to get a tractor driver to replace Raymond's father 18 months or so later. It appeared that all the potential tractor drivers around the area knew of his cantankerous ways and miserly wages and even a lovely modern home would not entice them to work for him.

The driver of the truck retorted. "All right for you Mister smartarse, we managed a load yesterday and this will take the rest of it, then we'll be gone, so you can bugger off and leave us to get on with it."

45

The farmer went bright red, puffed up his cheeks before telling them, "This is my land and you have no right to be here so you can bugger off now." Then he turned to Raymond demanding, "What are you going to do about your pigs. I'll give you a fiver apiece for them and take them off your hands now, so let that be an end to the matter."

Raymond replied, "You must be as daft as you think I am. Them, there pigs is worth 5 or 6 times that much .so get lost. If you really want them have a look in the Farmers Weekly magazine then decide what they're really worth." The lorry men were enjoying this interchange and were waiting for an explosion. The farmer strutted off up to the farm buildings then returned shortly afterwards.

This time, he started in with, "Now look here. This my last offer. I'll stretch a point and pay you a tenner apiece, so that's it. What do you say to that, eh?"

"No, get lost. A week ago, you tried to steal them from me for a fiver for the two of them. I know they are worth at least thirty quid apiece and no less. You go and have a good look at the pigs then make a reasonable offer and we might be able to do business."

"You're mad, you'll not get that for them. Look here, I'll give you 15 quid each for them and no more." Retorted Mr. Fernleigh as he pulled out his wallet to make the payment.

"Ok, Mr. Fernleigh, what you're saying is, you'll pay me 30 pounds for the pigs that are in the pen in the orchard, as is, where is, no questions asked." Replied Raymond.

"Aye well; it's daylight robbery and you well know it, but here you are then there's your 30 pounds, and they'd better be worth it." He gave him six crisp, five-pound notes then stumped off again.

The furniture men finished loading up and were preparing to leave. Raymond gave the money to his Gran for safe keeping. Just a final check-up and they would be away. Raymond on his bike, Granny would walk to the bus stop on the main road and the men were ready to climb in to the lorry. At that moment Fernleigh returned shouting for them to stop. He was beside himself with rage. He reckoned the pigs had gone, the pen was empty, and the gate left open. Raymond asked, "Was the little gate from the field to the orchard fastened shut as usual."

"Aye it was, and so was the big gate at the far end, but there were no pigs in the orchard anywhere."

"That means you've got no worries then. The pigs can't get out of the orchard, even if they got out of the pen. They'll have pigged out on all the windfall apples and will be lying down under the hedge somewhere. They'll have a massive belly-ache and be in real pain tomorrow but they'll recover."

"No, they won't. They're gone I tell you, the pens empty, so give me my money back now."

"Someone must have pinched them. I bet they're already in one of your pig boxes in the barn and out of sight. You must think I'm stupid You must have stolen them. No-one else could have come in here and moved them out of the orchard without you seeing them. Your dogs would have gone crazy if there were any strangers about. So! Where have you hidden them?" Raymond asked.

Fernleigh stepped up to Raymond and hit him a massive clout across the side of his face. Raymond would have fallen down but Fernleigh's other hand smashed into the other side of his face. Badly stunned though he was Raymond lashed out with his heavy work boot and kicked the farmer in the shin. As the farmer was forced to bend down as a result of the kick, his face came within reach of Raymond's fists. Raymond's brain seemed to have a mind of its own because of the pain, and imminent danger of further attacks, and it went into overdrive. He balled up his fists and smashed into that angry face. His little fists smashed around and around in a blur like the vanes on a windmill. They broke his nose, causing blood to spurt out, as the fists continued to destroy that hated face. He knocked out at least two of the farmer's top teeth in a gushing of more blood. Then he loosened some of the bottom teeth and carved up the lips and cheeks. It took only a few seconds before the lorry drivers managed to get a hold of him and stop the onslaught. Both sides of the farmers face were badly damaged and swelling rapidly. Both eyes would be closed due to the swelling and would surely be black as coal by morning.

Raymond walked over to the nearby cattle trough in the field in front of the cottage and swilled his hands and face. He held his nose and lowered his face deep into the cold water of the trough and this seemed to ease his pain slightly. When he was running short of breath, he raised his face clear of the water to enable him to breathe again. After a few deep breaths he repeated the dipping once again. He repeated the dipping action quite a number of times, holding his breath as long as possible each time, then he washed off as much of the blood and snot as he could, jumped aboard his bike and rode away furiously, without looking back. He was terribly upset and huge tears were pouring down his face. Thank goodness this was the last he would ever see of this hateful place and the odious farmer.

His Gran and the removal men were flabbergasted. They could do no more than watch him riding furiously away. The removalists left the half tarpaulin cover rolled up across the tail board so that the assistant could ride in the back sitting on one of the families arm chairs thus allowing Gran to ride in the cab with the driver and away they went never to return.

The lorry first went to Granny's house and dropped her off, together with a number of boxes of things that she was hanging on to, mainly family photos and trinkets. They also contained all Raymond's personal clothes, books, and other possessions, as well as some boxes of crockery and kitchenware that she was keeping, then carried on to the warehouse to unload the family home. Some of the belongings of the family would be offered for sale immediately whilst some would need to be held in reserve, in case it was needed later, by Raymond or his Granny, or to get a more favourable price once the dust had settled.

Raymond's face slowly began to heal with his Gran administering her favourite medication, sweet tea, aspirin, and lots of Eliman's Embrocation to soothe his bruises. After only a few days of treatment Raymond was getting over the shock and some of the pain. It was bad enough losing his Parents and sister without the added trauma of his beating. He still had two black eyes but he was feeling a lot happier when they received another great shock.

Mid-afternoon one day, there was a knock on the front door. Raymond went to open the door to welcome their visitor expecting his Aunty Libby, who lived nearby with her brood of kids, but it was one of the last faces that he ever wanted to see, peering at him through the open door. Horror of horrors, it was Mr. Fernleigh senior, the farmer's father, who presented himself. Raymond lowered his gaze to the floor and prepared to close the door in the man's face. In the past Raymond had loved and admired this old man, who had always treated him with respect and kindness when he was helping his dad and the Boss in the harvest fields. Every day the old man visited the harvest-fields. He always had two of his best eating apples in his jacket pocket, which he gave to the boy with a little ceremony and a huge smile. From a very early age, Raymond had driven either one or the other of the two big tractors from stook to stook, when loading the sheaves for carting back to the Dutch barns for storage.

As he was closing the door in the man's face, the man raised his arm and held the door open slightly before saying, "Please Raymond, may Mrs. Fernleigh and myself come in for a few minutes. We will not hurt you in any way, nor cause you any undue stress, but we really must sort out this mess before it goes any further. If at any time you feel too distressed just say so, and we'll leave your home immediately.

Raymond stood aside allowing his visitors to enter. He led them through into the living room and introduced them to his Gran. He announced, "This Gentleman is Mr. Fernleigh senior and Mrs. Fernleigh his wife." Grandma. Then he turned around pointing out that this lady is my Granny on Dad's side.

"Aye well I'm pleased to meet you both" said Granny. "Please sit down and tell us why you're here. If you're here to chastise my boy or cause him any upset you can leave immediately. You have a damned cheek even coming here at all, after what your crazy son did to Raymond here. How did you manage to find us anyway?"

Actually, it was the neighbour Mrs. Tranter who gave us a clue, and the furniture chappie did the rest. The furniture van had the owner's name written on the side of the cab, and the neighbour remembered it. We went down to see her, in case she had witnessed what had happened that day. She admitted that she was peeping through the curtains and watched the whole debacle. She told us that my son, Robert, smashed Raymond with a vicious blow across the face, followed by a second blow on the other side of Raymond's face, knocking him to the ground. She then said, that when Raymond regained his feet, he kicked my son on the shin as hard as he could, causing him to bend down in pain and stick his face in the boy's face, causing Raymond to attack him and defend himself from further blows. We spoke to the removal men, and they confirmed the story stating, that it was definitely my son who struck those first two vicious blows.

Mrs. Fernleigh took up the story, telling them that their son was infuriated, and looking for vengeance. He needed to equal the score, and bring Raymond down to earth with a bang. He had told them, (his parents), that he could not let this outrage go unpunished. He is going to take any steps necessary to avenge this crime. He is also seeking compensation from you to cover his medical bills and loss of face. He will need to have a false plate made to repair his teeth. As you know Raymond Mr Fernleigh and myself have always respected you, and welcomed you into our lives, so we decided to make sure of the facts, and reasons behind the facts, to make sure that your good name is not unfairly dragged down into the mud. Would you like to tell us your story and please cover all the relevant facts and any little details that might help us to sort this out.

Raymond asked his Granny for the return of the bundle of fivers that he had passed to her during the altercations. Granny retrieved the money and handed it to him. Raymond said, "There you are please take this and give it to your son. If it means so much to a mean, greedy person like him, he can have it back, as I want no part of it. He always strutted around pretending to be religious. Pretending to be a Christian, but he only ever achieved that status for a few hours on Sunday mornings. Any other time he was a true villain, and should be taken to court for cheating the Government out of funds with his black-market scams, some of which he carried out on the Sabbath day, of all days".

"Stop there Raymond please" said Mr. Fernleigh. Raymond, would you please explain the meaning of that statement, because it seems to be very damning against our son." Asked Mr. Fernleigh.

"I'll try Mr. Fernleigh and I hope I have all the facts correct. I suppose Mr. Bryant, the cattle man and Mr. Broderick the cow man are the only two people who can substantiate my story now that Dad's gone. As you know Sir, the ministry of food controlled all food supplies for the duration of the war, and many years thereafter. Meat was one of the last remnants of the food rationing system. Whenever there was talk of food inspectors in our neighbourhood, your son told the cowman,(who, often, enlisted my help), to hitch up one of the horses to each of the night arks and tow them down into the lower field, out of sight among the hedges and trees. They usually contained between 30 and 50 cockerels each, that were being fattened for market, especially at Xmas time. All the young growing pork pigs would be herded into the big fold yard, among many loose bales of barley straw. As you know, strange pigs don't mix well, and pandemonium would set in, with pigs running madly around and fighting like mad, and squealing their heads off. We lads were told to run in among them and pretend to help count the blighters. In desperation the inspector would accept the reduced total that your son provided to him. The final act, occurred on Sunday morning, when my Dad and Mr. Bryant, with me helping, were feeding the fat bullocks in the back-fold yard, at the lower end of the Dutch barn. Partway through the morning, every Sunday morning, the local butcher would drive into the yard and reverse his horse box towards the gate. Mr. Fernleigh came out to join him, and when the gate was opened the box trailer would be reversed into the gateway. One of the best bullocks would then be walked over and loaded, into the horse float, the tail gate closed, and the butcher would drive off with his contraband. One Sunday morning the butcher reversed back too far and one trailer wheel dropped down the sleeper step into the manure. When the butcher went to leave, he couldn't move forward because the trailer had been steeply angled to the car to enable it to be steered into the narrow gateway. The rear wheels of his car had little hope of getting enough grip to lift, the now loaded, trailer wheel up the step. Mr. Fernleigh sought out my Dad and told him to start one of the case tractors, to tow the butcher out. Dad pointed out to him, that he, the boss, had always maintained that neither of the tractors were ever to be started and used on Sundays for any purpose what-so-ever, so he refused. Because your son is left-handed, he can never start the tractors on his own so Dad left them to it. He whispered to me, "The silly buggers haven't the brains to reverse the trailer further in to the yard to straighten the car up as much as they can, then get a good run at the step" and bump up over it.

Sorry Mr. Fernleigh, but all this must partly explain why I have no love for your son, and he for me. As you know my dad kept a couple of growing pigs in the old yard at the end of the orchard, and your son thought that I would be stupid enough to, virtually, give them away to him. He came down to the cottage, when we were sorting out our final possessions, and berated us for still being around. He said he had told us we only had until the previous Friday, to clear the cottage, and clean it up ready for the next tenants, so why were we still there. He accused the removal men of trespass, but I told him that the cart track through the farm was declared to be a "Public right of way," and he had no jurisdiction over it at all. This was only a few days before the funerals of my whole family. He showed no sympathy with my loss, and never said anything nice about it, or my Dad, after 14 years of dedicated service for only minimal wages. It was still a few days to the funeral because we were waiting for the coroner to release the bodies for burial due to problems concerning the lorry design. He offered to take full responsibility for my pigs, and see to their removal. He offered me a fiver for the two pigs and expected me to accept such a miserable offer. When I refused to discuss the matter he very generously [his words] upped his offer to a fiver per pig. When I again refused to accept his offer, he stumped away, telling me I would be very sorry, because that was all they were worth."

On the following Tuesday, [let's not forget my family had only been dead for 1 week], we were loading the last of my possessions and were nearly finished, when he came down to the cottage again. Once more he berated me for still being there, and threatened to call the police unless I left immediately. What a nice way for a so called, Christian "gentleman," to treat a sadly bereaved, eleven, year, old orphaned school boy. Then he asked me what I was going to do about the pigs. As he said: I couldn't leave them in the orchard any longer, so I would have to sell them to him, or he would lock the gates and I would forfeit the pigs to him. He then offered me 15 pounds per pig and that was his final offer. I asked him, "Are you offering to buy all the pigs left in the yard in the orchard for thirty pounds."

"Aye, that's what I just said, thirty pounds and not a penny more," He handed me six five-pound notes and stumped off back to the farm. I handed the notes to my Granny for safe keeping and she slipped them into her hand bag.

We were about to leave, when he came storming back to the cottage, claiming I had robbed him. He tried to take the money back, but as I had given it to Gran for safe keeping, he couldn't get hold of it. He claimed the gate had been left open, and the pigs had gone. They were nowhere to be seen. So, I said to him, "Don't worry me about your pigs. I don't own any pigs, and any left in the orchard are yours, as you purchased them fair and square, and they are your responsibility. That's when he stepped up in front of me and smashed his big tough hand to the side of my face then followed that with another savage hit on the other side of my head. Stunned though I was, I remember getting my balance again and kicking out at his legs. I remember no more until the furniture men pulled me away from Mr. Fernleigh, and stopped him trying to hit me again. I washed my face and hands in the cattle trough nearby, got on my bike and left the farm. I have no recollection of hitting your son and if I did, he deserved it." I would like to add, if I may, I deeply regret that I allowed a good, so called "Christian" person, to infiltrate my brain, and coerce me into the dreadful actions that I apparently took. I probably should have been strong enough to just walk away from such a terrible affront, instead of resorting to the same tactics used by a Christian Gentleman, like your son. In the bible it clearly states that, if a man hits your face you should turn the other cheek but he had already hit that side as well. What I did was a reflex action. I never intended to hit your son, and I never even thought about such a retaliation, or that I could ever carry it out and get away with it. He is much bigger and stronger than me as you will be well aware. It never entered my head that I would be able to hurt him. I just reacted automatically as a reflex reaction to such severe pain that I had no control of my actions."

Mrs, Fernleigh was having great difficulty trying not to laugh out loud but she stood up moved around the table threw her arms around Raymond and burst into tears as she hugged him close. When she let him go Mr. Fernleigh took over and he was shedding a tear or two as well.

Mr Fernleigh waited until most of the emotion had settled down, and Gran had brewed a pot of tea. As they were sipping their brew he said, "Ok young Raymond I'll accept your story because it tallies exactly with the tale that the other three witnesses have told. That only leaves one issue to be resolved, Raymond. Do you have any idea what happened to your pigs? Do you know where they are now?"

"Yes and no to that Mr. Fernleigh. I sent the pigs away to market whilst your son was at church on Sunday morning. They were auctioned on Monday morning and I have no idea what happened to them after that. The auctioneers paid me 65 pounds for my two pigs. "Both of the Fernleigh's burst out into uncontrolled laughter until the tears poured down their faces and Gran and Raymond joined in. Mrs. Fernleigh picked up the fivers from the table and handed them back to Gran, telling her to put them away out of sight, love. Which she promptly did, "Saying, Aye, well that's grand, it will see us through the next week or two, lad.

When we find a suitable school for you it will mean new uniforms and other clothes."

At that point the Fernleigh's prepared to depart but before leaving they assured Raymond that their family lawyers would sort out all the mess, and he was able to assure Raymond and his Gran, that he would see to it that there were no repercussions from any these matters. Finally; he said that if they ever needed any help about this or other matters they were to telephone or call at the house. He said to telephone their home as soon as they had details of the funerals, which Raymond promised to do.

Before departing, Mr. Fernleigh said to Raymond, "I must tell you that although my son only paid your father a minimal farm labourer's wage, he was worth much more than that. Your Father was very clever at fixing machinery and keeping it going when something went wrong. My son is going to regret the day that your father died and left him without his expertise. He knows that your Dad will be difficult to replace and he's very worried because its harvest time, and your Dad will be sorely missed, and much of our son's reaction was due to that fact; but it doesn't excuse him taking it out on you. Mrs. Fernleigh and myself are quite devastated by the loss of your father, and if you ever need anything in the future, please do not hesitate to call us. If; when, you find a suitable school, or college, you must give us a telephone call and we will buy you a new uniform to start you off in style."

Raymond was dreading the day of the funeral but it had to be faced. A large Humber limousine arrived at the due time, and drove them and his Aunty Libby, to Clifford village, where the Catholic Father, Mother Superior and the nuns took charge. Raymond was delighted to see the older Fernleigh's waiting in the church but not, surprisingly, Fernleigh junior, his dad's old boss had not made an appearance. The auctioneers and their families, as well as the office lady, were in attendance also, and they loved and cuddled both Raymond and his Granny. Before leaving the auctioneers explained to Raymond that they had sorted out the mess with the lorry dealer and the manufacturer. They gave him details of a bank account from where he could draw limited emergency funds until the courts had finished, and assessed the amount of compensation due, which they had assured him would be very substantial, but would take a little time to assess, even though the guilty parties had pleaded guilty as charged.

Chapter Three

A New Beginning

After the Fernleighs departed, Raymond once again scoured the classified advertisements in the Yorkshire post newspaper. Under the heading, "Education". It was only a small insert but might be the solution they were looking for. It announced a secondary day college just off Honstent Road and near Meadowbank drive. That meant that it was close to the railway station and bus terminus, and only about 15 miles from Granny Clarke's home: "his home" from now on. There would be a long walk at the school end, but he could apply for a free bus pass to reach that point. He could get off the bus at the junction between Board Lane and Honstent Road. leaving a decent walk to the college. In summer that would not be too much of a deterrent but once winter settled in it would be quite a serious obstacle. The Leeds bus stopped close to his home at Granny Clark's leaving only a short walk after crossing the road to and from the bus. His new home with Granny Clarke was situated just inside a large estate which had been used by the Canadian Air force during the last war. The houses were very basic but had decent ablutions, bathrooms, and gas hot water systems, as well as gas cooking stoves. These facilities alone had considerably eased his Granny's work load, because the previous council house had coal fired hot water, cooking and heating, making a lot of extra work for the old lady. As a bonus, the bus stop was close by saving her much walking back and forth with her gammy leg. There were two small bedrooms,

The college people were advertising for extra students, with eleven plus certificates, to fill their classes for the current year. Back in Leeds apparently; a new high school had been built further south towards the Huddersfield road, and quite a lot of students had transferred to that school to reduce travelling times, and thereby leaving substantial vacancies at

Kingston College. Early the following morning Granny and Raymond hopped on a bus and headed for Leeds city. The bus conductor explained where they were best to alight from the bus, leaving a minimum of walking for Granny Clarke.

They enquired at the reception office of the college, where all their details were collated and logged, before a meeting with the Dean of the college. The Dean welcomed them, and after a very satisfactory interview, Raymond was accepted as a suitable candidate. The main obstacle of course, was the distance between college and the Leeds bus route.

Back then to the reception office, where they discussed the cost and availability of the appropriate uniforms, and other supplies needed by students, and means of obtaining a bus pass, if it came to that.

Whilst discussing uniforms and the cost of them the secretary had a sudden recollection. She said that an elderly lady had dropped in to see her some time ago, explaining that due to the sudden death of her grandson, she had a full set of new uniforms, and other items of interest, to dispose of. She supplied the details and telephoned the lady mentioned.

Mrs. Osbourne, was the lady in question and she was keen to meet Raymond and his grandmother. She lived some little distance away on a large farm. The grazing land had been leased off leaving a substantial area of gardens and orchards, as well as a large heated greenhouse. To help his Granny, Raymond used a little of his money to pay for a taxi ride, which the secretary organized, to get them to the farm.

The farm was within reasonable cycling distance to the college. The farm house was a massive Georgian mansion comprising three levels of accommodation and cellars as well as attics. The elderly lady welcomed them into her home and had already set out morning tea with sandwiches and cakes which were very welcome. The lady's tales of woe were almost as traumatic as Raymond's, and fairly recently, she had lost her only grandson, and his father in an air crash in Austria, leaving her without any relatives at all. She was an only child and her daughter-in-law had died in the childbirth of her second child. Her son was working overseas as some sort of diplomatic officer and the lady had taken over the care of her grandson a very early age. Only in the last few years her husband had died quite suddenly from an undiagnosed pancreatic cancer, so she was left with young Andrew and the farm. Her next-door neighbour was running a large dairy operation and needed more grazing land, so she leased him most of her land, which conveniently adjoined the neighbour's own farm. He supplied her daily milk, cream and eggs, on top of the lease money, so she was well set up.

Her son, preferred to have his son educated in England, so he had travelled back to Yorkshire as often as possible, to spend time with him, and renew fatherly bonds. Last summer however, he was unable to leave his post because of political disturbances around the area where he was stationed, but he did manage a short sojourn in Austria for his holidays. He arranged for his son to join him there for a couple of weeks of the summer holidays, and the small plane they were travelling in developed engine troubles and crashed into a mountain side, killing all the occupants.

After enjoying morning tea, and listening to the lady's dramas, she took them for a tour of the house, much of which had been closed off for years. Her grandson's room remained untouched since his demise, except for regular cleaning by a daily help lady. She had studied Raymond's height and stature and decided that he was almost the same as her Andrew. Andrew had been killed during his summer holidays therefore the school uniforms were brand new, as were most of the other clothes She began pulling various articles of clothing from a spacious wardrobe, and encouraged Raymond to try them on. They were a little on the large side but only marginally so.

They tried to talk to Mrs. Osbourne about prices, but she would not discuss any of that, so they went down stairs again and she led them out into the garden, which was huge. It contained a very large heated greenhouse which was almost derelict, and had been little used for some time due to the age of the gardener. There was an extensive orchard containing apples, pears, plums and even some cherry trees. Nearby, there was a badly neglected soft fruit grove with gooseberries, raspberries, loganberries and strawberries. All the orchard and gardens were in a mess. There was so much pruning, weeding, manuring, harvesting and other duties awaiting some energetic person to attack them. Raymond turned to the two ladies saying, "Oh what a pity, my dad would have made a really good living off this lot, and he would have loved it, but unfortunately, he's gone now."

Apart from the large amount of farm buildings, there was another substantial house near the driveway. and Raymond asked Mrs. Osbourne about it. She said that it was fully furnished of sorts but was now empty. She had employed an elderly gardener for many years, but he was now domiciled in a home for the elderly because dementia, or something, had settled in and he needed full time care, hence the garden was a disaster. Raymond and his granny put all that information aside for further consideration.

Mrs. Osbourne led them back inside and prepared to put a nice lunch on the table in the dining room. Raymond helped out with setting the table and preparing for the meal. Mrs. Osbourne went into the kitchen and opened the oven door of the Aga cooker and pulled out a decent roast beef with vegetables set all around it. She carried it into the dining room and placed it on a wooden board ready for carving. She asked Raymond if he was any good at carving, which he said he was, as he picked up the carvers and ran the steel along the blade a few times. She told him there was no need to be miserable he could cut nice thick slices. It appeared that she had prepared the roast early in the day when she was warned of their pending visit. She declared it was a real treat to have company to share a roast meal with, instead of eating it all alone.

When the meal was finished, and more tea consumed, she asked them if they were interested in the clothes and uniforms. Granny said they had to get some clothes from somewhere, and these seemed to fit nicely so it was down to money, like how much because they had limited finance at the moment.

Out of the blue, without any preamble, Mrs. Osbourne asked Raymond, "How would you like to live here with me, you could have Andrew's old room and his uniforms and clothes as well. It would be much easier to get to college, and there's a nice smart racing bike in the shed. It would probably need the tyres pumping up and a good oiling. Raymond and his Gran were stunned. This would solve most of their problems, but they needed to find out about the money, before they could think about a deal. Once Raymond's insurance money, and any compensation came to hand, they would be able to cope, but until then it was all impossible.

Mrs. Osbourne said, "That is the least of your worries because I am quite well off and have a steady income from the farm lease. All that aside, I am a lonely old widow. I miss Andrew so much that it hurts and you could maybe fill that gap. Now that Hubert has left me, I need someone to work in the garden, and you, young though you are, seemed to understand what is required. If your Granny is happy for you to live here with me, it would benefit all of us.

So, what do you say to that young man? Do we go ahead and give it a go? We will soon see if it works out and you can always move back to your Granny's, and take the uniforms with you, if you are not happy here."

Raymond said in reply. "This is all a bit much to take in at once. Do you mind if I go outside into the garden, while I think about it. There are so many things to consider. I won't be long and you can have a good old natter with my Granny."

He stepped outside and strolled around the garden, and had a good look inside the greenhouse, which eventually, led him to the other house. The outside looked fine and in good shape, but inside, that was another story. The whole place smelled of neglect and damp but that was easy fixed, just open a few windows for a start. The kitchen cum living room was truly huge, but it really was a dreadful mess, but easily fixable with a lot of elbow grease and hot water. He wandered throughout all the rooms, and it was obvious that they had all been unused for many years by the look of them. There were four good sized bedrooms upstairs and a large bathroom, with a separate toilet. Old Burt must have slept down stairs next to the kitchen to save his old legs. Off the vestibule, there was a small bathroom and toilet as well as the laundry, on the outer side of the passageway. On the other side a single door led into another large room similar to the kitchen which had obviously been a family room, because, there was also a comfortable lounge room at the front of the ground floor. Burt had turned the family room into a large bedroom cum sitting room, complete with a double bed and some odds and ends of cupboards and drawers for his clothes and other paraphernalia. This room would nicely house Granny's furniture and effects. At the front, opposite the lounge room, there was a formal dining room complete with a nice set of furniture, and a thick layer of dust. There were attics above, and a huge cellar below, and a hot water system in the slow combustion stove that might still operate once the fire box was cleaned out and relit. The ideas were coming fast and furious now. Raymond wandered back to the house, hoping for a nice cup of tea to wash the dust out of his throat.

After a nice drink, he posed the question to Mrs. Osbourne, "Have you decided what you're going to do with the other house, Ma."

She gave him a little chuckle at the term of endearment saying, "It really is a terrible mess, but basically sound. Have you thought of something in this short time, Ray?"

Just a few early thoughts, Ma, and if you are agreeable, and others keen, I reckon, we can make something of it. Gran might howl me down of course, but if she wanted it, we could really make it special. What I wondered is; if Gran could move in there on to the ground floor, where Burt has been living, after we get it cleaned out and habitable that is, I could keep an eye out for her in her old age, and she could pay you the council rent from where she is now. This farm is close enough to the shops, and if we could get milk and eggs from next door, until I get some laying hens. That would only be a start because the place is so huge a whole family could live there. Aunty Libby lives next door to Gran on the council estate, and she and Gran are quite used to living on top of one another in spite of all their kids. Uncle

Fredrick works in the city here as a builder and brick layer and it would save him heaps of time, and bus fares if he lived here. He could help out around here, and help with repairs and renovations, and repainting inside and out. They could both pay their current council rent money to you. The rent that they are paying to the council isn't very much, but if you got both lots it should be plenty, when added to the repair work. Even the kids could be persuaded to help me get the garden working again."

"Ok Ma, a lot to think about all round, but if Gran is happy, I would love to move in with you here, take over Andrews room, and his belongings. I promise that I will respect all his things and do enough work around the garden and greenhouse to repay you for my keep, and I will respect you, and your property so that you never, ever regret what you are doing for me today, thank you very much for this generous offer. Can I call you Ma instead of Mrs. Osbourne. I'll return home with Gran now and sort out a few things and move in tomorrow ready for college in a week or two. if you are ok with that. It will be a few weeks before I start college because we need to get the funerals out of the way and sort out all our finances."

Gosh Raymond, you don't mess around or waste words do you. Yes of course that's ok. Let's do it, and do please call me 'Ma', I love it. That was Andrews favourite name for me."

They were about to order a taxi but Mrs. Osbourne insisted on driving them back to the bus stop in her Austin A40 shooting Brake. Then she had another idea by suggesting, "I could run you both back home in my car, and collect all Raymond's bits and bobs, instead of him trying to fit them on his bike, or the bus. He probably won't need his own bike, but he can ride that back here sometime so he has a spare."

'Gosh Ma, thank you for that, because, I've got quite a lot of books and my huge meccano set, that I like to have around me, it's just shoved under the bed, with all the books heaped up in a corner of the room, and they would be a nightmare on the bus."

Back at his grandma's place they had a chat over a cup of tea and Gran decided to give notice to the council and move into the derelict house. The question of what to do with any furniture and effects that belonged to Burt had to be discussed, and Ma suggested that they continue to use anything that was useful, and the rest could be stored in one of the old farm buildings for now, or up in the attics. After all, Burt would never need any of them again and she'd not been able to find any relations of his who might like to keep them and use them. She said she'd searched through all the papers and documents in his house, very limited though they were, but there wasn't even a Xmas card, or a birthday card from anyone.

Before Ma and Ray returned to Leeds, they walked round next door to have a chat with Aunty Libby, and explained about the house. She was very excited about the idea and promised to discuss it with his uncle Fred. pointing out that their council house was far too small for them now they had four kids, two girls and two boys, and only two bedrooms. The oldest girl Paulette, was almost eleven now, and needed a room of her own. They had to leave it at that but everyone was quite excited with the proposed move. There would be more than enough furniture in the upper rooms and attics to house the whole family in unaccustomed comfort. Both Gran and Aunt Libby needed to give notice of one month, to quit the council houses giving them plenty of time to sort out their furniture, and other effects, and repaint any of the house that needed attention. With Uncle Fred being in the building trade, they could make it very comfortable indeed. On that Saturday morning the whole family, Gran as well returned to Leeds to inspect the house and have a chat with Ma.

Raymond hadn't had much time but he had removed lots of rubbish from the down stairs rooms and lit a bonfire in the garden to burn anything combustible. He cleaned out the slow combustion stove and lit a fire in the firebox, to check out the hot water system, which was soon bubbling away happily. The heat from the stove and fresh air through the windows soon improved the atmosphere throughout the house, so he kept it burning coke, day and night for the rest of the week.

Once the house was much more habitable, Ray concentrated first on the greenhouse, then the rest of the garden. There was a neglected crop of tomatoes in the hot house that needed tying up` and pruning as well as a good watering. It was almost too late to harvest many tomatoes, but a good watering and a snitch of fertiliser, the plants responded well. Raymond told the ladies that any which didn't finish off nicely they could make up into a green tomato relish or chutney. It would need a few of the small onions, and a few spices to make a good brew.

Soon the weekend was upon him and he was looking forward to spending most of his time resurrecting the garden. First however he had to plan his non-daylight hours to get through the weekend's homework assignments as well as trying to catch up with the lost tutorials due to the funerals and moving houses. He was determined not to let the trauma of these last few weeks curtail his education. He discovered amongst Andrews possessions a full set of text books from the college which he had been swotting up on hoping to be only little below the other class students when he started. Even though it appeared that he could make a good living around home, he was aware that a GCE certificate would make a useful addition to his CV.

Uncle Fred really liked the idea of living close to work. He said that quite often the weather interfered with their work and it would be a great help to be able to work half, or at least part of a day, instead of losing a whole day's wage, due to a few showers. Also, Aunty Libby loved the idea of being nearer to shops and Paulette would be able to attend the college because, apparently, she was very bright and certain to pass the eleven plus examinations. Whilst they were there, they all got stuck into clearing out the surplus junk and beginning the massive clean-up. Ma lent a hand from time to time and she loaned them her vacuum cleaner, and other cleaning gear. By the time that it was time to catch the bus home, they had organized one of the ground floor rooms for Gran as a bed sitter, and the rest of the ground floor was habitable They had laundered most of the linen, towels etc, hung the blankets outside to blow the dust off, prior to organizing a dry cleaner to bring them up to scratch.

When Gran got back home she went for a trip to Tadminster to see her furniture removal friend to organize him to move her belongings He told her he was holding quite a lot of cash from the sale of the family furniture and there was enough to pay for her removal to Leeds and more, and he would drop off plenty of boxes so she could start packing. When she was ready to move, she only needed to ring him and he would do the rest He said Monday morning was best for him so she told him to come around on Monday next, which he did. Aunty Libby and her brood pitched in to help her clean the cottage ready for the new tenants. She left the keys with her daughter with instructions to hand them in to the council offices on the due date. Once she was installed in Leeds, she set about getting the bedrooms ready for the kids and her daughter. Any time the weather prevented Fred from working he turned up to help prepare the new home, and sometimes he even brought one or more of his workmates to help. The whole family began sleeping in the house at the weekends to allow more time to prepare it for them to move in.

The kids insisted on travelling on the bus after school on Friday afternoons and camping in their new home, with Ray keeping his eye on them. They would need some of their old furniture as soon as the carrier could deliver it and install it, and they needed to empty the council house quickly to enable a good clean-up of the rooms, prior to handing in the keys. The smell of the new paint was off putting but it would soon disappear.

Ma was already spoiling Ray with kindness. They both needed a lot of solace to eliminate all the horrors of the past couple of years. Ma was also missing old Burt's company during the daytime, but the weekends were making up for some of that. She pitched in to help the family get comfortably settled and the kids were keen to help weed and prune some of the garden and berry orchard.

Aunt Libby's kids were having a ball. They had never lived out of town, nor had they had this much freedom. They were willing to help out in any way they could. Paulette was only a year younger than Raymond, then there was a large gap to her brother Phillip who was eight years old. Next there was Lynette with Bobby, the 'baby,' at nearly five years old. The whole family, as well as Gran, settled quickly into the house, which was soon fully furnished with selection of assorted furniture, including some of Burt's accumulation, and oddments from Raymond's old home, intermixed with some of his Gran's antique bits and pieces, with the remainder belonging to Aunty Libby. The family had found quite a lot of furniture and fittings in the attic and some of it was quite good, so the furniture removalists took away any saleable items to cover the cost of rehousing everybody.

As soon as Uncle Fred managed to get the house comfortable, he went with Raymond to inspect the greenhouse. The structure was in reasonably good condition needing mainly a lick of paint and a few new panes of glass. The interior was a mess when Raymond first saw it, but he was slowly getting on top of it with some help of sorts, from the kids. They discovered a quantity of ripening tomatoes far more than they could use themselves, even after making batches of relish and chutney.

Ma Osbourne remembered a small wooden stall that her husband and old Burt had used outside the front gate, to sell surplus crops to passers-by. A serious search of the old, stone, out-buildings, soon located the stall and everyone chipped in to clean it up, paint it and set it up on the roadside.

The stall was an instant success because many of the locals remembered it from long ago and were keen to be among the new customers. Ray searched through the gardens and orchards looking for items to sell and there were plenty, including rhubarb, apples, pears and other fruits, as well he found a large patch of potatoes buried among the weeds. They had regrown a new crop without any help from Burt and needed only to be dug up and sorted. Also, in the weeds, there was a large plot of shallots and some self-sown onions. There was also a large area of culinary herbs. They discovered heaps of parsley, mint, sage, thyme, dill, and some chives. They were in business.

What they needed was a more permanent supply of vegetables and fruit so Paulette began checking the adverts in the local papers and they soon had a good supply of seasonable vegetables and fruit. In reply to their own wanted adds, they located quite an assortment of produce, much of which they were required to harvest themselves, therefore, mostly free of charge. Apple trees keep on producing without any help but a number of older people were not agile enough to harvest them. They realised that the hedges were loaded with blackberries so everyone pitched in to harvest them and soon they had friends from school volunteering to join in the work. Evenings and weekends were fully booked, picking, digging, cutting and harvesting. Ma used her Austin A40 to collect and deliver the produce and Fred recovered an old derelict van from his boss. It was a bit dilapidated and needed some love and attention, having been neglected for many a year, but it ran nicely once a new battery was fitted and the oil changed. The kids found a row of hazel nut trees, growing along the edge of a woodland area, which Ray and Fred harvested using an old wooden ladder, which they discovered in one of the farm sheds, because many of them were too high for the youngsters

89

to reach. Life appeared to have taken a turn for the better for young Ray and his immediate family group. Living with Mrs Osbourne, or Ma as he called her, was extremely pleasant and much of an improvement on his old life. Sure, there was plenty of work for him, but he was his own boss, driving himself incessantly in any direction he pleased, within certain limits. This was soon to change somewhat as college loomed before him. The day to day drudge of orderly school life did not please him but needed to be tolerated until he could obtain his GCE certificate. The vegetable stall was proving to be an unqualified success as he acquired new sources of product and supplies, and a good many regular patrons as well.

Chapter Four

Training College

The first day at a new school are always traumatic for all except the most outgoing kids. For Raymond this first day was to be doubly upsetting. He was a few weeks late in getting started due to sorting out the family business and moving to a new home, even though settling in had turned out to be quite easy, thanks to Ma and Gran. Any school or college, was always going to be a problem because he was a total stranger in this neck of the woods, and knew none of his fellow students, who had a few weeks start on him, and already begun to 'mate up', as you would say. Ray walked into morning assembly feeling lost and traumatized, but he had to make this part of his life work. The headmaster announced that Raymond needed to attend him in his office immediately afterwards.

The headmaster welcomed Raymond into the college and handed him an assortment of papers to quickly peruse. He pointed out that his college wasn't quite like an ordinary grammar school, where pupils were gathered into defined groups and forced to attend certain set curriculum. He was told that he could, to a certain extent choose the subjects which suited his ambitions and life style, although some subjects like mathematics and English language were mandatory.

"So! Raymond, looking at the lists before you are there any subjects which appeal to you, or as more often is the case, subjects which you may not wish to participate in? You can begin with the basic curriculum and adjust it at the end of each term until you find your way."

"Thank you, Sir. much of this is quite alien to me, but I'll try. Firstly, as you suggest Mathematics which is so important as is the ability to write and converse articulately, so they must be a starting point, and if I intend to run my own business, which I do, they are essential. I do already enjoy both Mathematics and English hence my top pass marks in the eleven plus exams. I'm going to be actively involved with horticulture, which I love, and sales and presentation of the produce, much of which I have set underway already. To these ends I need a good knowledge of chemistry and biology and maybe physics. I see you cater for metalwork, which will help me to repair and modify my machinery, because I need to learn to weld and braze metal, so add that, and woodwork to the list. Foreign languages are not necessary at this point in my life and can be added later if needed. Also, games and gymnastics are totally irrelevant as I will be active enough at home. I see you do not cater for more practical subjects like horticulture but domestic science would be useful, to enable me to experiment with various recipes to better use my produce and crops, and maybe teach others to do that. I really enjoy cooking at home anyway and domestic chores are a serious part of my life, now and in the future."

"Well done Clarke, that is a good selection to get you started, but domestic science might be a problem. You probably realize that it is basically a girl's only domain, and you would be the only boy in the class. I will need to discuss this aspect with Miss Jones, and if she is ok with the idea, we can certainly give it a try. Who knows, some of the other lads may even want to learn how to run a home efficiently. They may even aspire to becoming professional cooks, bakers or chefs. One more point which could be important to you is the daily timetable. We have the ability to vary attendance time to suit the needs of students who live a distance away from the college, and in view of your home duties, we may be able to reschedule your days, to allow you more time before and after classes."

"Yes Sir, that would help me greatly, if we can organize a suitable schedule it would be appreciated. I will be doing a good deal of my studies outside class as well. If the afternoon, for example, ends in sports periods or other classes that I will not be attending, I would like to be free to leave as soon as my last class of the day is finished. One point I need to make, is that I intend to try and arrange afternoon and evening classes, at the agricultural and technical colleges on Walter Lane, if they have suitable subjects, which you do not cater for. This means that I may need to be flexible enough to work between the two colleges to save time."

"I am stunned, Clarke. You are really serious about all this and I am sure that I and my staff, will co-operate as much as possible, good luck with all that, and keep me in the loop as much as you can. Thank you for this input and you can get along to class now. Call at my secretary's office now, and she will work out a timetable to suit you and organize your first class."

The first class available was mathematics, and Raymond was supplied with the current text books for the course. He was quite surprised to find that he had very little, if any, catching up to do, because he had been studying Andrew's text books, he was ready to go. After the first class his fellow classmates welcomed him into their midst and promised to help as much as possible, especially when he told them of his mixed-up schedule. Ray coped well with the day's work and was allowed to leave mid-afternoon instead of taking French tutorials. He hopped on Andrews racing bike, which he'd put back into service, and headed for the technical college further out of town on Walter Lane.

Although further afield, the agricultural college was still within easy cycling distance, both from home and from the college. This college catered for most classes of agriculture and horticulture as well as vehicle repairs and maintenance, all forms of woodwork, art classes, plumbing, electrical engineering and many others provided lecturers were available. Ray soon located the general office and put in a plea to become a student. When asked what subjects were of interest, he studied the long list and picked out, horticultural science, practical horticulture, vehicle repairs and maintenance, basic electrical installation, plumbing, metal work, welding and book keeping, along with economics and business management.

The secretary was somewhat bemused but set to work arranging classes and tutors. Some subjects were quite simple such as book keeping, metal work. plumbing, and basic electrical. Vehicle repairs and maintenance had been held in abeyance due to lack of numbers, but his nomination confirmed that class as a goer. The horticultural tutor was contacted and he said the theory and science was ok, but the practical segments need suitable venues, such as parks and gardens, to provide sufficient practical work. Ray asked if the tutor could possibly meet him at his home at the weekend, where he thought there would be enough practical work to keep an army of students busy.

The course tutor Mr. Frobisher was astounded with the amount of work, some current, and lots more historical. He had 6 other students, four were girls, keen to become involved so he was happy to set up a class room in a loose box room close to the scene of action, ready to start pruning and training the trees and berry bushes the following week.

From now on Ray was going to be extremely busy but he was determined to make a success of this part of his life. Having grown up on a mixed farming enterprise and been force to help out, and work alongside the regular farm workers, and his father, proved to be a great start. Some of the subjects such as welding and general metal work overlapped with the college making his work slightly less arduous, but he needed to become very proficient in all aspects of the work, to keep his machinery up to date and working well. After working alongside his Dad, Ray started the courses with a very good working knowledge of machinery maintenance and repairs, but modern machinery needed to have welding repairs as well. He needed a good working knowledge of both oxy-acetylene and electric welding. He planned to buy an electric welder as soon as he possibly could. A firm called Lincoln Welders made quite an assortment of arc welders but new ones were expensive. The head tutor of the electrical department, Mr. Robertson, approached him with a suggestion. He asked Raymond, "Are you really keen to get an electric welder Raymond?"

Ray replied, "You bet I do sir. I have a number of repairs to my machinery already that need some welding, and I have some basic designs for modifications, as well as new machines, especially for small properties rather than the big commercial designs. I can't drive, and don't have a vehicle, so I can't take the machines to the blacksmith shop, and I'll need to do a bit of welding, try it for size and fit, then weld again. I really do need to have a welder of my own."

"Ok, that's great so why don't you build one yourself. It is quite simple and cost effective. The best type of welder is a D.C. welder, because they penetrate much deeper to make a stronger weld. We can go to that big salvage yard on the Bradford road, and should be able to get what we need. How about I pick you up on Saturday morning and drive you out there, so we can see what he has available."

"Are you saying that he will have a welder in the yard, Sir?"

"That's not very likely, but we can make do with other machinery. It will be a useful exercise for the whole class to be able to design and build a complete working machine starting from scratch, and it will save you a heap of money."

'Ok, Sir, how much money will I need if we find something useful?"

"Oh, not very much if we are lucky. Do you have any spare cash just in case?"

"Yes, I can use my petty cash reserves, or I will have to draw some more out of the bank account next Monday if needed.

"Right you are then Raymond, I'll call for you about 10 o'clock on Saturday. In the meantime, I'll set each member of the class to work, to see if they can design the basic structure."

The stall was always busy on Saturday mornings so Ray had to get up extra early to organize the produce and staff. The older ladies volunteered to 'hold the fort' to help out, and there were a few high school helpers ready to dig up, or harvest various crops as needed.

On the way to the yard, Ray ask his tutor why he was doing this to help him. Mr. Robertson replied, "Because it will make a good practical experiment for the class, which will be much more beneficial than working on inanimate objects, which they will not have any useful benefit when complete"

At the yard they found a few 32volt generators recovered from heavy wartime bombers. The biggest. one had enough output for the job and nearby they discovered a rheostat, voltage controller, which would enable the output current to be adjustable for different jobs and electrode sizes. Both items would need a good deal of cleaning and tidying up, but that would be good experience for the students. He only had to pay scrap metal prices to obtain them.

There was an old scrapped car chassis on the farm and on one old farm machine they discovered a PTO drive shaft to suit the Ferguson tractor. From all this scrap the class welded up a framework to carry the generator, and current controller, and brackets for a counter shaft. The bearings, suitable belt pulleys, and belts he bought new. Also, they decided to replace the universal joints on the drive shaft. Safety guards had to be fabricated from old car bodywork and weld mesh. The framework was fitted with a tow bar made from the old chassis to hitch it to the tractor. An old axle and wheels added underneath, to make it into a crude trailer for towing it around. Eventually the class put all this waste material together and produced a neat, workable welder, for very little cost to Ray. A tin of industrial primer, undercoat, and finishing paint was used to put the finishing touches to the welder. Getting

101

enough long, flexible, copper leads was a bit of a trial, but finally overcome after a couple of visits to the scrap yard. He had to buy a new, hand piece, and a face mask to go with the electrodes.

That enabled him to weld other bits of scrap metal together to produce a simple machine for lifting potatoes and carrots. The digger was quite slow but he could lift small quantities of potatoes each day as required. An engineering firm in Oxford built a small sickle mower with two very large diameter wheels, which he modified using a much more powerful motor, retrieved from an old motorcycle, Ray and his class members modified all that along with odds and ends of old machinery both on his farm and neighbouring farms. The whole thing was very crude but it took much of the work of getting the spuds from the ground and separating the spuds from the rubbish and dirt. Particularly early in the season when the potato skins were thin and fragile much care and gentle handling was needed to minimize skin damage which would cause the potatoes to become green and toxic.

Ray hopped on his bike during the week for a tour of the scrap yard. The manager was surprised to see him again so soon. After helping him with his afternoon tea, Ray managed to fill in some of the blanks. He told the manager, Jeffrey, that he needed to pre heat pieces of steel and other metals. He was looking around for an Oxy/acetylene welding outfit and possibly some sort of forge, or bits to build one. Jeffrey told him, "Come and have a look at this, it would suit you well for a start," but, it will cost a lot more than you might expect to pay. It's in near new condition with all the welding nozzles and cutting tools, a large preheating torch, and it came on a trolley." Parked in the shed there was a full set of Oxy welding and cutting gear. Just what Ray needed. "How much?" he asked,

"You may well ask young man, but although a bit pricy, its well below the cost of a new one if you're interested, and I'll deliver it for you free of charge, so what do you say?

"I say well done Mr. Jeffrey. When can you deliver it?" Ray asked.

"How about tonight, after I close up here if you have the money?" was the stern reply.

Ray grabbed his hand and shook it vigorously. Ray then reminded Jeffrey about a forge, or bits to build one, and was told it might take a week or two, but he would find something.

Although it was almost too late for the current season, Ray was thinking about a much better type of ladder for working on the fruit trees like apples and pears. The ancient wooden ladders were quite dangerous and unwieldy. He went to his favourite scrap yard again looking for ideas and inspiration. Jeffrey gave the matter a good deal of thought, then told one of his men to take Ray over against the back fence. There they had dumped lorry loads of scrap metal recovered from an American air base. In among this junk there was what looked like a portable staircase. It was very difficult to extract the structure made of galvanized water pipe. The original wheels were missing but it was otherwise complete. Apparently, the ground crew had used it for repairing the aircraft. One end had had an axle from side to side, with two wheels to move it around. The other end only had two curved plates to stand it on. It was easy to raise the end without wheels because the position of the axle allowed the framework to nearly balance thus the ladder could easily be moved around by one person. The axle had been welded onto the frame away from the end allowing it to balance and make it more manoeuvrable. The steps were quite large platforms to hold bags of fruit and the top step was a reasonable sized platform with hand rails on three sides. The handrails had strong hooks attached to hang tool bags onto, which would be ideal for fruit bags. This was almost perfect for pruning fruit trees and also for picking fruit. Ray walked around the corner to a car wrecker where he knew there were a number of wrecked cars. The wheels were equipped with useable tyres and the class only had to carefully bore 4 holes in each hub to match the wheels and they were in business.

There were still some apples and pears to pick, and a massive, pruning sessions to follow once the leaves dropped off, so the new machine would get a good workout once finished.

The tutors were looking forward to working with Raymond throughout Autumn and winter.

There was enough practical work to keep everyone busy, any time they had to spare.

Ray was keen to try out new pruning techniques to improve growth and harvesting. There were a number of different ideas floating around but the older trees did not lend themselves to much of it so new trees were the answer. Ray asked his horticultural tutor, if he could help him select more suitable varieties and growth styles, to create a more workable orchard. He pointed out that there were a few acres, unused at the moment, which he could work up and plant ready for spring. His tutor was delighted and organized a trip for the whole class one weekend. He drove them to an Agricultural Research Facility, where he knew the instructors, having trained with them himself. The result was plenty of new trees some old varieties like Bramley seedling and some new, experimental varieties. The college was keen to unload the Bramley trees to comply with the EEC rulings, so they ended up with enough dry-rooted trees to complete the new area. They also received a good selection of soft fruits, and berry fruits, like gooseberries, loganberries, and raspberries. Fortunately, some of the compensation money had been deposited into his bank account and there was a lot more to come. The life assurance company had also deposited a large sum of money from his parent's life policy, most of which he was quite happy to invest in new trees.

Once back at home, it was all hands-on deck to be ready for the tree delivery, as soon as they were ready. They collected loads of manure from the dairy farm next door, ploughed it in deeply then marked out the tree lines, Ray managed to buy a stack of off cuts of timber from a nearby sawmill to support the trees, and erect trellises to shape them. Once again, the college jumped in with the woodwork classes, designing and erecting the frameworks.

The following year Ray was offered a young, partly trained, cattle pup, a lovely welsh collie, whose owner had become too infirm to carry on with the training. He said he didn't want any payment for the pup, but reckoned it had to go to a good home where the training could continue and the pup would be loved. Ma Osbourne approved the idea although they had no live stock to need a working dog, but she realised that Ray needed a companion. Once the pup, FLASH, arrived, Ray began setting aside mornings and after school hours for the training. The adjoining dairy farmer, Mr. Fairweather, was delighted to help out, and allowed the pup to bring in his milking herd twice each day. This proved to be an excellent training ground, because the cows had a set routine morning and evening. Soon the pup was bringing the herd in unaided and marshalling them into the byre. Once the farmer opened the gates, he sent the dog away on his own, with just a whistle, to collect the cows and bring them into the yard.

Ray loved this little welsh collie and they got on so well together. His dog would sit still, waiting for the command, then take off at speed to complete the task. They were never apart for long, the dog following his every move except when he had to attend college. The interaction between Ray and his dog, led to another association that was to prove long lasting and very rewarding, not only for boy and dog, but also for a nearby farmer.

An elderly couple were farming straight across the road from the fruit stall, where they ran a herd of beef cattle, which were beginning to become too much for the elderly couple to handle. One Saturday morning, Ray looked up from the stall, to see Mr. and Mrs. Metcalf running around the cattle out in the field trying to get them into the yards. There was much shouting and yelling but the cattle were unused to being handled, and shied away each time they got near to the yard gate. Ray could see the old people were knocking themselves up, Mrs Metcalf particularly, and getting nowhere. The noise and activity had Flash stirred up and on edge, straining at his lead. Ray asked his Gran if she could watch the stall for a while so he could help the Metcalf's. He called flash to heel and walked over the road to help. As soon as he gave the word, flash took off to round up the cattle, whilst he suggested to the thoroughly exhausted, Mrs, Metcalf that she might like to go back to the house and put the kettle on, because they would all be ready for a drink of tea once the cattle were in the yard. She thanked him gratefully and went off to do just that.

Flash quickly had the better of the cattle and soon had them all puffing and panting as they trotted into the yard. Mr. Metcalf closed the gate behind them, then began thanking Ray, but Ray was having none of it. He said all the thanks were due to Flash, without who they would not have got them into the yard. They left the cattle to cool off and settle down as they walked up to the house for a well-earned. drink. He asked the farmer for a bucket or something to give flash a drink but he was too slow. Flash took a flying leap and landed in the stone cattle trough for a dunking and a long drink, he jumped out and shook himself 'dry,' with a big grin on his doggy face. They all went inside, except flash who was still dripping wet, for a welcome cuppa and some freshly baked scones. Afterwards Ray ran across the road to his home but promised to return shortly after checking the stall. His Aunt Libby was officiating by then, with Granny helping out. They were really enjoying playing shops and consorting with the customers so he left them to it and returned with flash over to the Metcalf's place. A team of youngsters were acting as backup to the ladies; digging up and harvesting various crops as the ladies began to run short, collecting eggs, and weeding in between times. Ray had acquired a useful group of high school pupils who were looking for pocket money, and who were available weekends, holidays, and sometimes morning and evening. He had spent many frustrating hours sorting through the youngsters to put together a reliable group. Quite a number of the kids thought it was just a playground, and only wanted to mess about, and come and go, when it suited them, throw broken carrots, cabbage stalks, and clods of dirt at one another.

Meanwhile, back over the road, Mr. Metcalf explained that there were two mobs of cattle mixed in together because someone had left a gate open. The larger Hereford cattle needed to be shipped out and sold but the little black angus were to stay for another year. Ray suggested that Mr. Metcalf take charge of the gate, whilst he and Flash sorted out the smaller ones. The bigger cattle were pushing the little ones out of the way as they tried to hide deeper into the back corner of the yard, thus pushing the smaller ones out into the open yard and out of their way, so it was easy to separate most of them, and shunt them through the gate back out into the field until next year. There were only a few now left to be separated, leaving the big ones ready to load for Monday's market. Ray said to give him a shout when the lorry arrived, so Flash could load them for him. As you would expect Mr. Metcalf was extremely grateful for the help, mainly from Flash, of course, and a little from Ray.

They all returned back to the farm house to clean up, and drink more tea together. Raymond decided that now was a good time to sort out another item of interest that had bothered him for a while. He asked Mr. Metcalf what they were going to do with the apples and pears in the orchard and around the garden. Frank Metcalf said he was too old to pick them and had no use for them anyway; so, if Ray wanted them, he could help himself but he would need to pick them off the trees. Ray was delighted because he was running low on fruit at that time. He told them about his picking platform and offered to prune and tidy up the trees later to pay for the fruit and lay claim to the following year's crop. Frank was delighted with that idea. He offered to let Ray use the huge vegetable garden as well. so long as he kept them supplied with a few vegetables as a reward. All this was very agreeable and there was a heap of old manure by the byre and pig boxes to go with it.

Ray was shown into one of the old stables where odds and sods and bits of old machinery were stored. Amongst it all there was what appeared to be a decent sized, self-drive rotary-hoe which would be extremely handy, especially now he had all the extra garden areas to work. Mr. Metcalf dampened his spirits somewhat when he mentioned that the engine was stuffed. It had always been a brute to start, he said, and finally impossible. It had not been started and run for over a year. Also, the whole machine was long overdue for new tines and a general clean up and lubrication. The gear boxes were in dire need of oil change and adjustment, ready for work.

Raymond decided to enlist the aid of his engineering class to overhaul it and improve the starting. The instructor was delighted to have a practical project for the class to work on, and with his supervision, the rotary hoe was completely reconditioned like new. With a few simple parts the magneto was quickly put into working order, and so was the carburettor, the class even cleaned off all the rust, prepped the metal work, and spray painted the whole machine, which looked like new again. It was a Howard built, rotary-hoe and parts were still available through a local dealership. He would need a full set of tines, and bolts to mount them, as the existing ones wore away. Mr. Metcalf then guided him around and into a large stone barn saying, "Come in here pal and have a look around, I'm sure there'll be plenty of machinery that you'll find useful, especially this Ferguson tractor. There are many attachments, and some machinery to go with it, if you're clever enough to work out how to get it started, and how to use it. Like the rotary-hoe, the tractor hasn't been started for a long time, so it will need a new battery and a good service before you can use it." The Ferguson tractor was much more sophisticated than the case tractors that his dad had used, and much smaller and more manoeuvrable for garden work. it was fitted with three-point linkage lift at the rear, making it much handier to operate. As a bonus it had a power take off drive and a flat belt pulley drive to work with the welder. The Ferguson tractor at Mrs. Osbourne's farm was similar, but a fair bit older, and he had managed to get that one working well enough, although it was short of implements and accessories. In the barn, Ray found a 5-foot rotary hoe to fit the tractor

Ray was delighted to have the use of all this equipment, so he quickly ordered a battery and was able to start the engine. The following day he was due at the college and suggested to Mr. Robertson that the engineering class might need another commercial enterprise to test their skills and he accepted with relish. The class serviced and repainted the tractor and much of the machinery as well. Ray was delighted and made another donation to the college funds by way of saying thank you. He could now begin to establish a large extension to the orchard and berry fruit garden at Metcalf's property. He organized the horticultural class to go with him to the college near Beverlay, to obtain the latest trees and shrubs to plant in the orchard. They offered to assist once again with the planning, planting and espalier erection. The tractor got a good workout ripping up the ground, cultivating and manuring it ready for the new trees.

It was about this time that Ray became aware of a new line of sprays suitable for agriculture and to a lesser extent horticulture. A firm who specialized in developing, manufacturing and distributing chemicals had set up business and were canvassing the agricultural scene to spread the word. A representative of the firm called to see the farmers of the area to tell them of these new, wonderful advances, deemed to make farming easier and more profitable. Ray viewed the information with a lot of scepticism and doubt. and because there was no follow up information to be had at that time, he decided to wait a while. The range of chemicals being offered included insecticides, fungicides and weed killers. He was a bit interested in the insecticides and fungicides to protect his crops. He needed to control mildew and fungus attacks around the fruit trees and vegetable crops. The hot house crops were constantly in danger of mildew and fungus. He worked out that, if he took all the precautions, gloves, face masks etc. and sprayed early in the morning there was little probability of any side effects. The insecticides, which would be handy, would put his bees at risk especially with the flowering crops. The agent suggested that he could spray certain crops like peas and beans at day break before the bees were active but Ray felt any residual chemical left on the flowers would be a danger. He did some experiments with fungicides which were a great help in the hot house. The insecticide he decided to stay away from. Later that year there was an article in the newspapers about two dead spray men a few miles north of his place.

A well to do farmer was experimenting with alternate crops and planted 20 acres of field peas for stock food. They were troubled by a moth which laid its eggs in the flower buds. When they hatched the grubs, or cut worms, devoured the young pea seeds and ruined the crop, so he called up the chemical firm to have them sprayed.

Two men turned up the next day with a wide spray boom and suitable chemical. The job was finished by lunchtime and the men sat down alongside a haystack in the lowest corner of the field to have their lunch. It was well into the afternoon when one of the farm workers realized that he hadn't seen any activity in the field for a fair while. The field was quite visible from the farm yard because it ran up hill from the road. The farmer had a good look out and agreed with his man that there was something odd going on. He sent his son on his bike to see what was happening

When he arrived in the gateway, the son, could see the spray men lying under the hay stack fast asleep, or so he thought initially. On checking them out however he was pretty sure they seemed to be dead. He'd never seen a dead body before but he couldn't rouse either of the men.

He raced back to the farm and told his Dad that he thought the men were dead. The boss climbed into his Austin A70 pick-up truck and drove to the hay stack. There he was soon convinced the men were deceased. He drove back home and rang the local policeman and left the rest to him. The policeman arrived and checked out the scene, before riding into the nearest village to alert the ambulance and back-up support from the police. No-one was ever sure, but it was thought to be either, the men had carelessly eaten their sandwiches with chemicals on their fingers, or because of the slope of the field the fog of chemicals had drifted down to the hay stack, or maybe a combination of both.

The incident proved to be a severe warning to Ray and all the other farmers of the district. The men had not been wearing rubber gloves, nor were they even equipped with them, or suitable gas masks, even whilst handling the raw, full strength, chemicals.

Chapter Five

The Fairer Sex

Aside from all the work and study Ray, was becoming aware of a certain amount of scrutiny, and snide looks from some of the young ladies now surrounding his new life. He had always lived on a remote farm with little involvement with girls, except for his odious sister who he disliked intensely. He and Georgina had never got on well together, although they never got into any physical fights only verbal ones. Georgina never showed any affection to her brother. She spent most of her spare time reading comics and girl books, although with her mother's help, and use of the ancient Singer treadle sewing machine she was quite adept at making and mending clothes. They had no common interests so it was impossible to engage her in any small talk, nature walks, or rambling around the countryside which he enjoyed, whenever his father didn't need him to work with him. Because of this, Ray didn't know how to relate to members of the opposite sex and since the demise of his family, he was so engrossed in sorting out his life and study routines, that he had little time for social enterprises anyway, but he could not completely ignore those around him.

One girl at the college seemed to be always making eyes at him, and bumping into him in corridors and class rooms. Her name was Melanie. who asked if she could visit the garden one Saturday morning and he naively gave her consent to do so. She knew where he lived, more or less anyway, because she had attended the pruning sessions with their class, and she lived close enough to cycle there one Saturday morning.

She arrived mid-morning, and was totally nonplussed when she saw the extent of the operation, due in part, to Saturday being one of the busiest days for the stall. There were a number of students working throughout the property, weeding, digging, harvesting and keeping the stall supplied with produce. They were busy rinsing the soil from root vegetables and trimming the leaves ready for sale. Poor Ray didn't know where to begin with this young lady so he left her to look around on her own whilst he concentrated on his work.

There was a steady queue of ladies waiting to be served, and the students were busy digging carrots, potatoes, and other crops. Another pair were kept busy carrying apples and pears from the storage shelves in the barn and the customers were buying up, mainly the Bramley apples, of which there was a large store in the barn, and there were still more to be picked across the road in Metcalf's garden and orchard.

At lunch time he invited her to join the others for drinks and sandwiches which his aunty Libby had prepared. He was finding his time with Melanie very pleasant and she appeared different in this environment rather than in college. He was finding out that she was good company, although naïve concerning the garden and stall, but because he was able to chat with her on his own terms about the garden, and the machinery, he found that he wasn't tongue tied anymore. He even began to ask her about her social life out of college, and her pastimes and hobbies. At the end of the day Ray began to shut the stall down and pack away the equipment and any unsold produce. Melanie was still hanging around and 'helping' to clear the area, putting the scales knives etc. into a nearby stone building, and cleaning the stall ready for the next day. She seemed reluctant to leave, but eventually hopped on her bike to ride home. Ray gave her a couple of eating apples still left on the stall, to take away with her, and she thanked him for them. Flash was a favourite with all the students and Melanie was spoiling him rotten. Because she, unlike the rest, had no set tasks she had plenty of time to walk around the garden and yard with him, stroke him, and pet him, and flash lapped it all up with glee. However; that did not please Ray. He pointed out to her that flash was a working dog, not a family pet, and as such it was not a good idea to spoil him. He realized that flash needed to be locked up in his quarters when there were youngsters about.

Ray had built a comfortable kennel for flash with a nice fenced yard surrounding it where he could relieve himself, get out and about as well as enjoy a little exercise. Nice though it was flash preferred to be free to follow Ray all day, which became a problem when Ray had to leave the property, or use the machinery.

Once the stall was cleared, he set about the task of organizing the stock for the following morning. He firstly went for a short walk out the back of the garden heading over towards the dairy farm with Flash at heel. He was desperately short of eggs for the morning and he had a deal with Mr. Fairweather to buy his surplus eggs at wholesale prices and sell them on to his customers. He collected the eggs each day, to sell fresh on the stall. He was going to need further supplies of eggs because demand was overtaking supply. As he was walking over to the dairy, he had an interesting thought. There was plenty of shed space over at Metcalf's place, so if he could obtain a hundred or so young hens, he could run them in deep litter in the old stables. Deep litter was one of the latest ways of managing laying hens. The floor was spread with a thick layer of chaff or sawdust and the hens stayed inside all the time. Raymond asked Mr. Fairweather if he knew where he could get a hundred or so pullets, or better still laying hens. Mr. Fairweather collected the latest edition of the Farmers Weekly magazine and the two of them sat down over a cup of tea and studied the adverts. There were a couple of possibilities. One commercial dealer had a serious over supply of young hens and pullets that he needed to dispose of quickly. He was equipped to deliver them in special crates, so, Mr. Fairweather negotiated a reasonable price delivered to Metcalf's place in the next day or so.

He arrived early on Saturday morning and Raymond had organized a load of sawdust from a nearby sawmill. He had help from his students to spread it out around the old stable and next door in the loose horse boxes ready for the hens. The man from PULLETS GALORE arrived mid-morning with the older birds, which they put in the stable with help from the students. He said there were definitely more than a hundred but not quite sure how many and Ray was to pay him for only one hundred as agreed. There were already quite a lot of eggs in the crates as they were emptied. There was plenty of room in the stable for that many and they were soon scratching around and making nests in the litter and perching on the stalls and laying eggs. Raymond had nailed some of the orchard trellis off cuts across the top of the stalls for roosts. Also, he had obtained a quantity of fruit boxes from a local greengrocer's shop which were ideal as nesting boxes.

Peter the pullet man asked Raymond, "Can you handle some point-to-lay pullets as well? I need to clear my sheds straight away so I can sterilize them ready for next year. I can go back and bring them now if you have room. They are already starting to lay, although the eggs will be a bit small for a week or two" Raymond showed Peter into the loose boxes next door.

He asked Peter, "Can I pay you for them on the first of next month so I can balance my budget"

"Ok, Peter said after a little consideration, but you won't let me down, will you. You will pay cash on the first day of next month won't you."

"Yes of course, just call at the house over the road and I'll leave the cash with Mrs. Osbourne if I am not going to be around. I'll send a couple of my helpers back with you now and they'll help you to catch them and get them into the cages."

Once again there were one or two eggs in the crates when they arrived although they were a little small being pullets. Ray took Peter across the road and introduced him to Mrs. Osbourne, who reassured him that the cash would be on hand on the first of the next month. Ray was certain there were more than one hundred pullets, but Peter said to only pay for that many since the school kids had done most of the work. Ray was also certain that he could easily sell all the eggs as well as Mr. Fairweather's eggs. Fresh eggs and other produce were always welcomed by his customers but of late he'd had to limit egg quantities due to lack of supply. Two of his hotel clients were making suitable noises so he needed to fill those orders if possible. Hopefully they would save the egg trays to pack the new eggs. Raymond with a little help from the woodwork class nailed together some of the thin, pine, packing, case boards to construct crates or boxes to hold six, two and a half dozen egg trays rather than the double-sided egg board ones. Containing 15 dozen eggs these were a good useable dimension for the hotel kitchens.

As expected by the principal of Raymond's main college, there was a backlash from other pupils who thought that Raymond's split class schedule should be offered to the other students. Some of the upper 3 years of students were allowed to follow suit with certain subjects that had tutors available. After a complete reshuffle new time tables were arranged, allowing the participants to eliminate certain subjects such as Latin, French and sports periods, as well as religious instruction. Ray had the opinion that religious instruction should, and must be carried out, and by the religious groups themselves not by busy fully occupied teachers wasting valuable school time.

As it turned out many teachers and colleges were in full agreement with this theory and were beginning to espouse it within the schools.

Amazingly, this idea led to a reasonable increase in student numbers, because some of the earlier defectors liked the sound of the new schedules and came flocking back for the start of the next term. The classes offered were mainly trade classes like metal work and wood work domestic science and the hospitality industry. To this end they encouraged local participants: hotel and restaurant owners, as well chefs, to endorse this theory, with a thought that it may possibly increase available candidates into their business, with training both in college and in their work stations.

One afternoon, as Ray was about to leave the trade college, Mr Robertson approached him wanting to run some ideas passed him. He suggested that Raymond should put some of his design and manufacturing skills to better use. Mr Robertson said, "Over the short time that we have been working together, Raymond, I have noticed that you seem to have ability to work around your daily problems, and often devise methods of making your life easier by designing tools and machines to assist you. I just wondered if you have ever thought

129

of designing and manufacturing some of these tools for sale. I believe you could work together with myself and some of the other tutors to improve, and in fact, perfect some of your inventions. It appears that little or nothing is being done to make life easier for small producers and home gardeners. We could involve our current class members and work together with a minimum of outside help to manufacture tools and equipment."

Raymond replied, "Well, what can I say. I believe we could do most of that and in fact have done some of it, but do we have enough machinery? We would, need lathes, milling machines and a blacksmith shop, just for starters?"

"Point taken Raymond. Have you considered subcontracting out the various jobs, ready for us to assemble, maybe in one of your barns, spray paint, and finish off, ready for sale. Initially we could retail them from your stall and demonstrate how efficient they are in your gardens."

"Yeah, well, all that may be possible in time, but I have very little of that at the moment.

I still have a great deal of studying to do to obtain my GCE. I'm working very long hours now with the stall, gardens, orchards and greenhouse. As you know I have recently moved into egg production in a fairly big way and I have contracted to run and harvest quite a lot of gardens and orchards around the area. Currently I'm using a fair amount of labour from students to help me but I will need more permanent workers later on. I haven't mentioned this to anyone else, but I have started to grow mushrooms in one of the cellars which may or may not be a goer. Both houses have large cellars and I have the use of the one over the road if I need it. If I think the mushrooms have potential, I'll need to produce suitable tables and stands to grow them, sort them and pack them so I would like to think the woodwork and metalwork classes might well be usefully employed. My biggest concern is to get the temperature and humidity in the cellars correct to encourage maximum growth, or indeed any growth at all. I have some available heat that is excess to the greenhouse and only needs piping into the cellars with suitable automatic

131

valves to control it. Only time will tell. Leave these thoughts with me Mr. Robertson and I'll mull it over during the next week or so and get back to you. I'll need some help from the plumbing class, to get the pipework ready for the mushrooms, if that is available from time to time." I'll also be needing a fair amount of support from the electrical class, to design and install lights, fans and thermostats, around the cellars, as well as upgrading the master switch boards to carry the extra load.

There was now a good flow of funds coming in from the insurance companies and compensation accounts so Raymond co-opted Mr. Robertson and some students to visit a salvage yard that dealt mainly with building salvage and was able to obtain quantities of water piping, second-hand radiators, and control valves, at scrap prices. This included a large amount of small piping that Raymond would have foregone, but Mr. Robertson pointed out that they would be excellent for building the support legs for the growing tables, as well as the mobile ladders. The radiators and some pipes were needed to increase the heating arrangement in the green house enabling Ray to extend the growing season and grow more exotic plants such as begonias to sell on his stall.

One day whilst he was working out the heating pipes, Aunt Libby came over to chat. She had the latest local newspaper in her hand and waved it at him as she asked him, "Have you seen the adverts in the latest newspaper Raymond? I've been studying the advertisement section in the local paper for many weeks and it's in again."

Raymond replied, "I took our copy in to Ma but I haven't had time to look at it. Why are you asking, is there something that you think might interest me in there?"

"Not sure. Not exactly sure but it might, if it's what I think it is, it might be worth you going for a ride on your bike to check it out. There is an advert in here for the sale of an apiary. It's been in for quite a lot of weeks now, and I think some people might think it's about birds and aviaries, but I think it is about bees. Have a look and see what you think." She handed the paper to him open at the page in question. He had a look and a big smile appeared on his face as he realised the implication of the advert, if someone else had not beaten him to the deal. Raymond asked his aunt, "What are you doing for the next hour or two, aunt, could you take over here for me so I can go and have a chat with this Mrs. Featherstone? It is a fair way to ride, but if I race there and back it shouldn't take too long, although it is in the hills and it will be hard riding."

"Look, pop in and see Gran and Ma, and between us we'll be able to manage until the kids come home from school."

"Ok Aunty, will do, and thanks for caring." He ran off to alert Gran and Ma, check his bike tyres and off he went. It was a hard ride right up onto the edge of the moors. He found the property without too much difficulty. He was about to knock on the back door of the cottage, when a voice called out from behind him somewhere. "Now then young man what are you up to. Coming to my place, knocking on my door? Can I help you with something or other? Who are you anyway and why are you here in my yard?"

Raymond turned around in surprise, to see an elderly lady emerge from a large stone barn across the gravelled yard. He replied by waving the advert which he had torn from the paper saying, 'It's about this 'ere advert Mrs. I wondered if I am too late. Maybe you have already sold your apiary."

"Nay lad, I suppose you are like all the others and are looking for birds. It's not about birds. It's about bees you see."

"Aye I know that Mrs, Featherstone that's what I'm looking for. I want an apiary not an aviary. I would like to set up my own supply of honey to guarantee my stocks. How many hives do you have and where are they? Can I have a look at them? Do you have the extractor and bottling equipment for sale as well?"

"Well you are a surprise one. Turning up here on a bike, of all things, and wanting to buy my apiary. I reckon you'll be hard pushed to fit it all on your bike, even if you make a good few trips.

"Getting it all home is the least of my worries. I have plenty of shed space to house the equipment and friends with vans and trailers to cart it there. Is it still for sale and how much will it cost? I have limited finance but I should be able to buy enough of it to get started." He said.

"Look young man, that's rather a lot to take in all at once and I reckon it will be easier if we have a cup of tea in front of us. I'm getting exhausted just listening to you, so, come on inside let's see what you're about. What did you say your name is?

"Sorry Mrs. Featherstone, I should have introduced myself, but you caught me off guard talking about birds. My name is Raymond Clarke, and I live on a farm off the Pontefract road. I have a busy vegetable stall on the side of the road and I sell jars of honey as well, when I can get them from people like yourself, but I would like to provide my own honey so I know where it comes from and also ensure my supplies"

"Oh yes, I know where you live now, I sometimes call at your stall for a few vegetables, mainly spuds. I've never seen you at the stall though, have I?"

"Not if you call during my school and college hours, my Granny, Aunt Libby and my landlady

Mrs. Osbourne attend to my customers during school hours".

They went into the spacious farmhouse kitchen and she pulled the kettle over the hob on the Aga stove and it was soon whistling away merrily. Once tea was brewed biscuits and slices of chocolate cake were added they sat around the table to discuss the details of the apiary. Mrs. Featherstone had collected a file of papers from a bureau in the lounge next door and pulled out a couple of sheets of paper. On them she had carefully listed everything that she wished to sell including 40 hives full of bees.

She pointed out that she was not keen to get away from bee keeping, but she couldn't manage moving the hives around to take advantage of the different seasons. She did have a crude trailer to transport the hives, although it needed running repairs, or in fact rebuilding, and maybe replacing especially if he was likely to move the hives further away. She said whilst her husband had been alive, he helped her with the heavy work but now she was on her own. She said that for the last two years she had not been able to move many of the hives around, and production had dropped off because of that. She said that it was really important to keep moving the hives close to the fields of flowers, to get the most from each season, and keep the flavour up to scratch. Different flowers changed the flavour such as clover, rape seed, and of course, later in the year, there were the moorland honeys. She pointed out to Ray, that the further the bees had to travel the less honey they produced, especially on windy days. Mrs. Featherstone said she had plenty of really good sites depending on the season, some on farms, and some on the moors ready for the gorse and bell heather flowering. She was certain that the land owners would be amenable to a change in operators, provided he was conscientious in his care of the land, and placement of hives. She said it was as much to the benefit of the farmers to get good pollination of their crops and fruit trees.

Raymond declared that he needed to get back to his stall but he was really interested and he would give it lots of thoughts and get back to her the following day. He said that, no matter what happened, he would work out a solution for her. He pointed out that, as, she herself had said, it was a heck of a lot to take in all at once.

Back at home Raymond took over the stall after restocking where necessary, and thanking his lady friends for holding the fort. A kiss or two and a good hug were all the payment needed by the ladies for a few hours messing about with the stall and its customers. Whenever the weather was nice the ladies, especially Aunty Libby really enjoyed the atmosphere around the stall. As she got to know the customers personally, she enjoyed a bit of a natter with some of them.

He had a lot of thinking to attend to and a plan of action, to work out, maybe with extra plan 'B'. He was considering some sort of joint plan initially with a view to taking over in total later on. Money wasn't a problem with all the funds now in place to compensate, as much as possible, for the loss of his family. He needed to keep the good will and site access, that Mrs. Featherstone had built up over the years, and build up a team to handle the extra work. Extraction and bottling were going to be a big job, whereas handling and moving the hives about was a simple straight forward business that he excelled in. He realised that if he could work a reasonable routine, he would need the engineering class at college to sort out and upgrade the transporters. Also, with bee keeping about to become part of his farming enterprise, would moving the hives around from site to site be a reasonable extension of his special driver's license, which enabled him to drive the tractor on the roads provided he was travelling between various parts of the farm scene.

With only a quick phone call in between it was three days before Raymond organised the time and staff so he was free to ride out and put forward a plan with Mrs. Featherstone. He proposed investing all the capital necessary to satisfy Mrs. Featherstone, but suggested that she might like to keep the extraction and bottling plant in situ for now, and he would spend as much time as possible with her around the hives, until he was quite competent in their management. He said he was quite amenable to her keeping a few hives close by as a hobby to amuse her and fill in some spare time. As they were going into Autumn and winter there would be less input needed there except repairing the hives and frames and preparing the sites ready for the spring flush of honey. He had spent some of the interim time talking to the woodwork tutor at the college and the students were madly manufacturing a quantity of spare boxes and frames to handle the honey comb. He explained to Mrs. Featherstone that they could take a quantity of the new boxes with them, when they went to collect the honey, and enough new frames to swap with the full ones. When the new boxes were ready, he diluted a quantity of honey and soaked the boxes and frames to remove the new smells of pinewood. He had managed to obtain 15 queen excluder frames to separate the honey combs away from the brood combs, and metal base dishes to catch any drips or dribbles. Mrs. Featherstone was delighted. She told Raymond that her husband had been thinking along these lines but never got around to it because he had no real interest in the business, and only looked on it as a hobby for her own amusement.

He arranged to meet early on Tuesday morning and go with her to the nearest hives and try everything out. She had a couple of extra hats and veils and Raymond had a zip-up boiler suit and rubber gloves so they were all set. The smoker was primed ready to go and she had tools in her Austin van. She helped him hook on a covered trailer to transport the, hopefully, full, honey boxes. At the first site, an orchard and clover field, there were six hives which were overdue for stripping. They soon got clobbered up and got into it. Once the hives were smoked, they checked each frame carefully to make sure the queen was in the lower box. The frames were swapped over for the new ones until the upper hive was empty. Raymond lifted the now empty box and its frames and Mrs. Featherstone, [Mabel], carefully fitted the queen excluder into place between the two boxes. Once replaced and the lid refitted, they moved on to the next hive. The new box felt very heavy, and Mabel was pleased as they transferred it to the trailer. All the queens were in the lower boxes, making it easier to fit the excluder. There was a small quantity of brood cells in all the upper boxes but with winter almost due the loss of brood was more a positive rather than a negative feature of their day. It meant there would be less adults to feed and nurture through the cold months when there were not enough flowers around to sustain a full hive.

So! Then it was back to base and extract the honey. Ray unloaded the full boxes and slotted them onto a table that was a good working height whilst Mabel boiled the kettle and brewed a cup of tea each for them. She plugged in a steamer to heat the knife used to uncap the honey combs and let the honey escape. Once the steam knife was hot enough, it was easy to sweep off the enclosing wax, and the honey began to escape as they were fitted into the extractor, and whizzed around at great speed to force the honey out of the cells. 6 frames fitted into the centrifuge and kept it balanced whilst it spun around. The frames were replaced in the boxes as they went along, and allowed to drip into the metal trays. Soon all the frames had been whizzed and extracted, and the honey stored in large containers ready for straining and bottling.

Mabel still had a large quantity of her usual labels to stick on the jars when full. With this batch being overdue, so to speak, she put plain labels on the jars, but explained to Ray, that in a normal year she was able to differentiate the various flavours and keep them separate. She explained that in a couple of days they would go for the next trip alongside the moorland to collect the heather honey which was special, and brought a higher price. Hopefully she could clear all the honey on hand before the heather honey arrived. She said the hives had been up near the heather for so long that it would be exquisite and exclusive at this time of year.

Ray and Mabel went through the process of getting the honey ready for sale, and filling some of it into jars and labelling them. Mabel loaded a good quantity into her van and delivered them for Ray. She was very happy to be able to keep supplying her most revered customers at her home, and staying friends with them. The following week she picked up Ray from his home, had a good look around the stall, and away they went up onto the edge of the moor, where there were 10 hives needing attention. They stripped the hives as before, and Mabel explained that there was still time for the bees to build up a store of honey, to feed the hive throughout the winter months. She told Ray that the following weeks they would refurbish the old trailer and he could help to bring them down home to his place to await the spring sunshine. He told her about the new trailer that he had designed and his tutor was presently welding it all together ready for next week.

Ray went around to ask if Mr Robertson had made any progress with the new metal trailer. He took some drawings with him to show his tutor. He had designed a gantry frame to bolt onto the chassis using another old truck chassis as a main frame, and an extending centre frame to slide out with a crane hook on the end. It was designed to hang a chain block from the hook, and he had designed a lifting grab, like a fork lift with two legs to hang from the bottom of the chain lift. The hanging point of the grab was carefully set up so that the hive would sit vertically and balance when hanging on the hook. The hives could quite easily be lifted up and slid onto the trailer chassis. It was long enough to fit 6 hives on board at once. The trailer axle could be moved back and forth so that the trailer balanced with a decent weight pressing down on the tow bar when the trailer was fully loaded. Once the optimum position had been ascertained, the axle would be welded in position. Mr Robertson suggested that they make two parallel overhead gantries instead of the single row but Ray explained that the hives were very heavy especially when full of honey so maybe 6 hives would be enough for now because all the hives went to different sites, except for the moorland trip where the hills would be a considerable drag anyway. Mr Robertson said the trailer would be ready for off on the following Wednesday or maybe Thursday, so Mabel would be able to fit it behind her van, and save the worry of the wooden one. Ray telephoned Mabel when he got home and arranged the new date for Thursday. The new trailer was, indeed, ready for Thursday morning, and imagine the amazed look on Mabel's face as she unhitched the old trailer and hooked up the new one. It was over an hour's drive up into the hills to the hive site. With some trepidation, Ray backed up towards the first hive and hooked the lifting frame beneath it and lifted it up slowly, carefully, but he had no need to worry, all went well. He was surprised to see that all the hives were closed off, and Mabel told him she had driven up the evening before, after, night fall and closed of the entrances. By lunch time the hives were unloaded near the orchard at Ma's place and the bees set free to work. After a quick lunch they were soon on the way again. By nightfall all the hives were in place, some at home and some over the road at the bottom of Metcalf's orchard and opened up again ready for morning. On Friday they started to strip the hives of their bounty and stored it at Mabel's place. Once more, they fitted queen excluders across the lower boxes as they finished each hive, and later in the day the wire worker delivered the remainder of the excluders. Mabel was practically exhausted,

147

and they still had heaps of hives to finish, and all the honey to sort and bottle.

Saturday was going to be a mad house because Ray had to attend to everything around home, open the stall, and there were customers waiting to be served, and it was still not quite 7.30am and his workers were still not on site. They usually got going by 8 o'clock so all was well, as one of his hotel clients pulled up his van in front of the stall. The new line in honey excited him and he picked up a box full of the jars and put them straight into the van, then itemised his vegetable needs. Ray weighed them up made out the invoice, and was handed a big fat cheque, shook hands with him and he drove off. Ray quickly went back behind the stall to top up the vegetables, just as some of his crew arrived. Among them was a middle-aged lady with a teenage daughter in tow, who he had never set eyes on, although the girl, about his own age looked familiar. Maybe, one of his classmates from school. He set the regulars to work then turned towards the unfamiliar lady, not sure whether she was a customer or possibly a potential worker "Saying, "Yes Ma'am can I help you with anything, this morning?"

The teenage girl was a bit bolder than her Mum said, "Please Mister, I've heard the girls at school talking, about working here part time to get a bit of pocket money, so I wondered if you had any vacancies for me. Mum here, would like to earn a little extra money as well. You see dad walked out on us and we need to make some money to buy our food and pay the rent, so can you help us?"

Ray replied, "You certainly came on a good day. Give me your names and you, young lady your age. As it happens something has just turned up and I could use two willing workers for today at least and maybe tomorrow if you are not religious. Apart from the work and wages, I'll see you before you leave and you can at least fill your larder with vegetables and fruit" He picked up a pencil and wrote down, Mrs. Margaret Taylor and Jenifer age 14 years. "Ok, now what do you know about honey?"

Mrs. Taylor stated "Only that it is sweet and nice and we eat quite a lot of it when we can afford it. Jenifer then added "I do sometimes go to Sunday school but I would prefer to work if you need me."

Ray spotted his cousin Paulette walking towards him so, he asked her to pop back home and get her dad, Uncle Fred to come down. He busied himself scribbling in his note book. Uncle Fred was stone deaf as a result of his wartime activities, so he had drawn a simple map for him. He asked him if he would kindly drive these two ladies to Mrs Featherstone's place and bring back any jars of honey that she had ready for sale, then he went into the house to ring Mabel, and talk to her about the two new ladies. Mabel agreed to give the ladies a start, but pointed out that she would not stand any nonsense from them. She said if they were prepared to work, it would take a big load off her shoulders because she was really bogged down at the moment. Mrs. Taylor and her daughter turned out to be willing careful workers, so they stayed all day until Uncle Fred was available to collect them, and bring them back, with another large load of honey, much of which was "Bell Heather" honey. Once the honey was unloaded and stored in the barn, Ray had a long chat with Mrs. Taylor. He asked her how it had gone throughout the day and she said she was very pleased with the way everything worked out. Mabel was lovely to work with, and although the honey was messy, they all worked together to minimise any spillage and mess. She said Jenifer had pitched in with a will but she was tired out now. Raymond asked her about the future. Was she available as a permanent worker, or was this just a fill in for her and Jenifer?

She told Ray that she was desperate to find permanent work so she could look after Jenifer properly. He took them around the buildings, including the mushroom cellars, and hen houses, as well as the green houses, and orchards. He pointed out that the outfit was quickly overwhelming him, especially, now the bee keeping and honey house was going to have to be slotted in, and as a result he would need a permanent employee who was self-motivated. He said he had so many roles to fill as well as college to attend, so she would need to come in and get started with whatever was the obvious need at any time of the day.

Opening the stall and getting it rolling along was most important, until someone relieved her of the responsibility, so she could go off and tackle the next most important problem. He said she would need to become competent with each facet of the operation, but especially the honey extraction and bottling, the egg production and Mushroom production. He said he had, generally, enough staff to handle the stall, and sales side of things during the daytime, and most of the harvesting was fairly well organised.

Margaret assured him that she had quite a lot of management experience having been 'foreman' in a large warehouse, and she could and would be able to organise her days between the various departments, and organise other workers to work with her.

That only left the sticky part; her. wages and extras. Raymond suggested that she could fill her larder with whatever goods there were around especially misshaped and damaged stock in the first place and quality stuff when there were no rejects. He said there is always plenty of odd shaped, eggs, mushrooms and other items which the market place could not capitalise on, that she was welcome to take home for their own use. Very small tomatoes, and berry fruits, apples, knobbly spuds, etc. that did not look good on the stall, would make her budget stretch out further and reduce the waste. Ray offered a pay rate that he thought he could sustain, although it was not quite as good as her previous wage, but the extras would certainly make that up nicely. Margaret accepted the deal as offered and was extremely pleased to get it, after months of struggling on the dole and other handouts. She added that Jenifer would be glad to help out at weekends to earn some pocket money, whenever there was seasonal work available. Ray replied, "We always need extra help at weekends especially Saturday morning and It would help if both of you are prepared to start at 6am. In fact; Margaret, how would it suit you to start at 6 am every day take an early lunch whilst we are a bit slack sometime between 10 and 12 noon and knock off about 3 pm.? When we are very busy you might even feel like working later for some overtime as well. I try to get the business

153

people to come in early so I can put in plenty of time with each of them, to introduce new lines and any special deals before we officially open at 8 am. I already have a few hotels and restaurants doing that and it seems to work well for us all, they get freshly dug or picked produce straight from the ground. Can you manage to get Jenifer off to college that early?"

Jenifer piped up, "No worry about that Mr, Ray I get myself up and ready without Mum's help anyway."

"Hey cut that out Jenifer, you're about the same age as me. Cut out the mister bit, call me Ray or Raymond."

"Ok Ray, sorry about that but you are our boss now, so I naturally added the mister bit."

"Ok then that settles that, I'll see you both at 6am tomorrow morning. I imagine you'll both be required at Mabel's for another day or so until you get the honey flowing nicely. Grab yourselves a carry bag and help yourselves to some eggs a bottle of honey and whatever you need in the vegetable line."

Whew that's a relief Ray thought, as he tucked into the basket of goodies and a billy of tea that his Gran had just sent over with his cousins, Kathy, Roger and Phillip. Prior to his discussion with Margaret he really was getting bogged down. The stall, and all the supply chain had suddenly become a serious business, that needed far more input than he alone could manage. He realised that only with good, constant management would any of his enterprises prosper, and return good solid profits. He was aware that he had been exceptionally lucky to be given all the help and encouragement that he had received, mainly free of charge, and it was up to him to make sure it paid off. He was also aware of the limitations of his Gran and Ma Osbourne. They were both getting past all this extra work although they were happy to help out, neither of them was capable of sustained input to keep the business going. The hens, bees, mushrooms, and green house, were constantly needing lots of input to maximise their potential, whereas the orchards and vegetables and to a certain extent the soft fruits could be delayed for a day or two.

It was time to shut down the stall for the night and Flash was getting excited. He knew it was time for a nice long walk. He was dancing around Raymond's feet and chasing his own tail in great delight. He had been neglected quite badly during the last few days, and was looking forward to making out with his favourite human pal. As the shadows began to lengthen Ray strode out along the road then turned into the fields to let Flash romp around at will. He checked out all the nice bunny trails and stuck his nose into their holes to say hello, chased around until he found a covey of partridge and sent them flying angrily across the field and over the hedge. Flash had had no stock work to attend to lately so he needed this strenuous workout to keep fit. He still brought in the cows for Mr. Fairweather morning and night, but that was only like a stroll in the park because they were so docile.

By the time he returned home and washed up, Ma was ready to serve up his dinner and discuss the day's events. She had been thrilled with the prospect of the bee keeping and honey business, and was delighted to be told about Margaret and Jenifer. Like Ray she was getting a bit concerned as to how he was going to manage to get all the work done each day and not drive himself and herself into the ground. Margaret, and her early starts, really were the answer to most of their problems. She and Gran could now relax and just help out occasionally if needed. Once dinner was over Ray settled into the snug, with Flash relaxing across his feet, there was a heap of book work to be attended to and incoming mail addressed. This was his least favourite occupation but it needed to be kept up to date. Whilst opening his mail he got quite a shock. The letter was from the EEC in Brussels. It informed him of the latest happenings within the EEC and informing him of his rights and of his obligations. He recognised this as the nightmare he was bound to have, like it or not.

They informed him of the need to fill in and sign the enclosed questionnaire. They wanted to know all about his business, what crops he grew, how he marketed them, details of any exports, details of all livestock held on his property, sales and marketing of them, breeding numbers and breeding statistics relative to breeding types, genetic details and

157

proposed numbers of offspring over the next two years. Without considering any restrictions, and reductions, and possible penalties, if he got any of it wrong, accidentally, or deliberately, just coping with the forms themselves would take up much of his precious leisure time. The only good thing about all this was his total lack of livestock except for a few pigs that he had acquired for their own use. He put it all aside for the time being and read the latest issue of THE FARMER AND STOCK BREEDER magazine.

Chapter Six

E.E.C. and Other Matters

It was Sunday evening a couple of weeks later that Ray decided to start work on the EEC forms.

He was quickly able to deal with the cattle, sheep, goats, deer, alpacas, llamas, breeding poultry, meat birds and horses. Laying hens, domestic pigs, and domestic poultry such as ducks, geese turkeys and one dog needed more attention. He had no grain crops, hay crops, root crops, and commercial potato crops. The form lacked a certain amount of definition which he would need to sort out when the inspectors visited the farm, as they surely would. He could not determine if the leased land was part of the survey and who was responsible for the crops and animals thereon. Similarly; the number of fruit trees and genetics of fruit trees was a real concern to him. He was not a landowner as such, so, did he need to list all the trees that he harvested on other properties. The mushroom business did not appear to be of any concern nor did the bee hives. He decided to return the forms that he had already sorted out as a nil return. They were in Mrs. Osbourne name not his so he got Ma [Mrs. Osbourne] to sign the documents because the farm was in her name and nothing to do with him, or so he thought. At a much later date he discovered that, that was not strictly true. After all he was not a commercial farmer as such. He was merely a backyard hobby horticulturalist. It was the stall which let him down in the long run.

As the stall became bigger and more expansive Ray had a good look at all the options. He needed to weather proof the stall for his own and his customer's convenience. One day when he was messing around in his favourite junk-yard he saw a covered lorry had been brought in and dumped in the driveway. It was really only a very large van with double doors at the rear. He asked the yard owner about the van and why it was in the yard. He was told that the van had been dumped outside the yard last weekend, and left there cluttering up the parking area. There were no identification signs on the van. The registration plates had been removed and the glove box was empty. It had to be removed quickly because it was a real problem for the yard.

The yard manager had no idea who owned it, and why it had been dumped in his driveway, so he rang the police station. The police did a quick search but found nothing to assist. They suggested that he drag it into his yard and cut it up for scrap. He and Ray had a good look around the van and realised the keys were still in the ignition switch. They tried to start the engine but the battery was dead. When they found the battery box under the tray body it was empty. They fitted a battery from the yard truck and soon realised that the motor was seized and useless. Ray said he reckoned he could use the truck at his place if they could move it that far.

George, the yard manager, offered to tow the van with his tow truck, which they did after removing the useless motor and gear box for scrap. Using Raymond's tractor in the driveway,

161

and the yard lorry behind, they managed to position it closely alongside the edge of the driveway, which was cut into the hillside leaving the raised section almost level with the lorry floor. There was a well-constructed stone wall supporting the driveway. The top of the wall was about level with the driveway surface making it level with the floor of the van.

George had to get back to the yard, he had wasted too much time already. The rear of the van was well clear of the road verge, away from council and police interference. When Ray offered to pay for the van and the towing, George suggested that he should be paying Raymond for disposing of the lorry. Ray asked about ownership papers and George got out his invoice book and wrote Ray an invoice and receipt for one pound. Ray had to give him a one-pound note to clinch the deal, which he did, meaning no-one could accuse him of stealing it. When his tutor called in later in the day to get his vegetables, he left his wife to do the shopping, whilst he and Raymond investigated the van. Mr. Roberson asked the big question, "Ok Raymond, what happens now, I thought you had plenty of stone sheds and buildings so what are you going to do with this old van?"

Raymond replied, "I was hoping you and the class might have the answer to that Sir, What I was hoping, is that we can remove the upper part of this side wall panel nearest to the driveway and hinge it to the top support frame to make it into a door. The back and front edges would probably need extra strengthening, fittings, and a flashing along the van's upper frame to keep the rain away from the top edge of the door."

"Come on then Raymond, where is your note book and pencil and we can make a start if you're free for a while? I suppose you're telling me that this is going to be your new stall, to replace the old wooden one before it falls to bits."

"I just need to run over the house and get Aunt Libby to stand in for me," Said Ray.

He returned quickly with clip board, pencil and eraser, they opened up the rear doors pinned them open and climbed into the rear of the van. Mr, Robertson said, "That will need to be the first job Raymond. A decent, rear, step ladder to save us climbing in and out like monkeys. Once inside they measured and sketched and scribbled.

"Ray, did you intend to open the full length of this side or only make it a window."

"I was hoping there would be some supports pillars along the side to support the roof and also attach the sheets, and look here, Sir, every two feet or so there is a dropper doing just that. Could we leave the first and last upright in place and cut the panel out from between them? We could build shelves in the end bits and join them across under the window to make a counter. The window would then be about twelve feet wide which should be plenty."

"Ok Raymond, what I would suggest is that you make two, or maybe three doors rather than one large one. That way you can leave every second pillar in place to strengthen the roof and support the counter, and the doors will be much lighter to lift up and down, especially if the girls have to manage on their own. Also, in rough weather you need not open all three, only one, or maybe two at a time.

Another thought Raymond, instead of building the shelves in the corner at the front we could build the shelving right across the front wall to allow for storage of extra stock.

"Heck yes, that's a great idea Sir. One long door would be too heavy for me let alone the girls. I say Sir, do we need to go for a trip to the scrap yards to see what we can dig up in the way of angle iron or better still that new style box tubing. We're going to need quite a lot of that, as well as extra sheet metal and galvanised flashing, hinges, lock bolts, and material for the shelving and counter. I suppose we might need to buy in a quantity of new material so it will look nice."

"Yes, I think that's the way to go if you can afford it and it will be a lot easier to assemble than old bits and pieces. I'll have to spend some time with my students to get them thinking about how it will all work out."

"Yes, I'll need some grey primer paint, undercoat, and gloss finishing coat, not to mention plenty of small welding rods. I've got the welder and air compressor running well now. Can you lend me your school spray gun or shall I buy one for myself?"

"They aren't very costly so I would suggest you buy your own, because you will need it, and a water trap and filter from time to time, to go with the compressor. We must make a visit the second-hand shop to see if they have one, and maybe some of the other stuff like locks and hinges. So, first things first, we need to measure up each window, draw the doors to fit the hole then work out the material necessary to make each door, A good idea would be to make duplicates of your measurements for me to take to college. Then, we need to cut out the sheet metal panels and cut away every second column to give access. Do you have oxygen and acetylene and a very small cutting tip then I can bring some of the class down here and work out how and where to cut the sheets etc?"

"Yes Sir, I have plenty of gas to get started and the small tip doesn't use much gas. What say you and I mark out the shape of the door before we get the class involved. Will we cut out a smaller square then bend the rest of the panel inwards to smooth out the edges. One thing I reckon we'll need to do is get the electrical tutor here with his class to work out how to bring the electricity from the barn then wire up the van for lighting and power supply, with fuses, and circuit breakers. Also, I'm certain we'll need a small sink in the back corner for hand washing etc, so we might need to get the plumbing class involved. That new-fangled black polythene piping will make it easier to connect it up to the shed. So! Mr. Robertson, can I leave all this for you, and the other tutors, to set up working classes for your students. There'll be plenty of skills, needed both mentally and physically, to end up with a very nice mobile shop. As soon as we know what materials are needed, I'll set that in motion for you. If I can manage half a day free during the week, I'll ride around to Sedgewicks second hand store and have a dig around. Who knows what they have in there, or in the big barn in their back-yard?"

"Ok then young fellow, that's enough to get you started, and we have a half term holiday the week after next so if you manage to get some of this stuff together we should be able to make a start and maybe some of the class might want to be involved as well. I'll go and see what my wife is up to before she buys you out of produce."

"That's a good idea and I'd better get back to work or I might get fired."

Back at the stall it was all systems go. He took over from his Aunt and Ma. Then, he got stuck into organising his staff. The two new ladies were already at full stretch so he organised back up to collect replacement stocks of eggs, mushrooms, carrots and most of the other lines. There was honey aplenty in the farm buildings, along with stored Bramley apples and spuds. Jenifer was shaping up well and helping her Mum. Melanie, had arrived so he sent her into the cellars to pick any mushrooms that were ready, and a couple of likely lads were dispatched, with a large trolley across the road to Metcalf's garden, to dig root vegetables, cut cabbages and cauliflowers. There was a huge crop of rhubarb over there that was overdue for harvesting, alongside parsnips, beetroot. leeks and onions.

It was during a break after the lunch time rush that Ray became aware of a looming problem. Both Melanie and Jenifer were trying to attract his attention and get as close to him as possible. He needed both girls working for him as they were both shaping up well, so he couldn't afford to have a war going on between them. Ray liked both girls, but having no prior experience of dealing, or co-habiting, with them he didn't know how to treat either of them. He knew that he might be able to cope with Melanie socially, on her own and maybe that would work out in the long term, or if he interacted with Jenifer where would that lead. He needed Margaret and she needed him so he couldn't try anything that would mess with that arrangement. The deal with Margaret was in its infancy but looked good at the moment. Because Margaret and Jenifer needed jobs, they might tolerate his nonchalance, whereas, Melanie, came from a more stable home background so, would she be more forgiving if things went astray? The answer seemed to be somewhere in between. Ignore, or at least just be nice, to both girls, but not become involved emotionally with either, and see where it leads. He really had so little time for a social life at that time so he only very occasionally went to the movies with his cousin, Paulette. He tried to keep the girls apart during working hours, with Melanie concentrating on Mushroom propagating and harvesting, and Jenifer working with the laying hens and egg production over the road. Both girls were worth their weight in gold and were quite prepared to pitch in with the others where necessary. Margaret apart from running the stall every morning, had a knack of foreseeing a coming need, and delegating staff to assist, to keep the stall fully stocked all day.

The work on the van went ahead in leaps and bounds during the half term break. They concentrated at the front, erecting all the shelving and extending it to become a counter along the side. The counter gave them a line to work to and they concentrated on the front window. The electrical class and tutor had connected the van up to the mains power, and fitted a row of fluorescent lamps along the roof, above the counter, and they installed 4 power points, which made the building and assembly work much easier, and they could work longer in the evenings.

The plumbing class only had one keen participator along with the tutor but they had little to do and they were finished in one day. All of the piping above ground had to be heavily lagged to prevent freezing during the winter months. So, they now had power and water. What a joy? The first window and door were soon finished and working well supplying a pattern for the other two, Once the first window was completed the next two were soon finished and ready to use. On the last Friday of the school break Ray and some staff members, began transferring the produce onto the shelves. Spuds and eggs were the first to come, along with carrots, celery and honey. On the Saturday morning, Ray was waiting for Margaret and Jenifer to arrive. He had opened up the centre window ready for business. The fluorescent lighting really looked good, and Margaret, with Jenifer's help, set up an exciting display on the counter. As the customers arrived, they were quite amazed to see the new shop. Ray had loaded the cash drawers with petty cash so they were soon in business. Ray progressively opened the other windows and the girls set up a great display of produce.

About mid-morning His Granny and Ma Osbourne came around bringing refreshments for all of the workers. Aunty Libby was not to be out done and turned up with a large chocolate cake with a thick layer of butter icing in the middle. Just then a man's voice called out, "Well, well, doesn't this all look very cosy. I hope you have another mug for a thirsty traveller.'

"Yes of course Mr. Robertson, although you are a bit early. The kettle is nearly boiled again, so hop into some cakes whilst you're waiting. Give us your honest opinion, what do you think about it now that it's loaded with produce?

"Quite frankly Raymond, I am completely astounded. Never in my wildest dreams did I expect it to come up like this. I must bring the students around to admire it. Most of the credit is down to them anyway."

"Sir, how would you all like to come around next Saturday afternoon, I'll set up a sausage sizzle for about 5pm and we can dance in the big barn next door. It only needs a good sweep out, and I have a radiogram with heaps of records."

"That's a great way of saying thanks to the students and maybe some of them will dig out some old Xmas decorations to make a festive scene. Oh gosh, I can't wait for that to happen."

Now Sir, seriously I owe you, your students, and the college, a great deal of money, to repay you for all this work, so I'll call and see the principal next week and make a juicy donation to the school social fund."

"Oh gosh no, that's not necessary Raymond. My students have benefitted so much with all this real engineering, rather than silly, imaginary, exercises. It has really explored their engineering and artistic talents beyond belief. However, if you feel that you ought to make a donation, the college will always make good use of it. Now, with all that out of the way I have a serious suggestion for improvements. I reckon if we carefully remove the rear off the old stall, and move the counter section across and behind the van, we can reinforce and strengthen it, to make a loading dock between the driveway and the rear doorway. A good deal of your stock arrives in wheel barrows, hand carts, and trolleys and, as you know, the rear door opens right around and lays flat against the side of the van. The bottom edge is high enough to clear the ramp, and we can add another layer of boards over the old counter top to make a walkway the same height as the ramp and across into the rear of the van, so you can wheel the barrows straight into the van."

"Gosh, that's a fantastic idea, Sir. I'll get started on it early next week. Thank you once again, I'm sure I would have got around to something like that, eventually. It's so obvious now the rest is finished. I'll talk it over with Ma, because her husband designed and built the stall years ago, and it might still have some sentimental value to her, although I had to dig it out of one of the barns."

The old counter part of the stall needed little modification, other than a safety railing, to fit it up as a loading dock at the rear of the van and with the extra boards across the top lined up with the floor of the van, and the boards increased the strength and stability of the whole dock.

Most of the customers commented on the improvements, and when the doors above the windows were set in the, near, horizontal position, they acted as a weather shield for the customers.

The van had been the "Stall" for a number of months and everyone was delighted, except for the local council who sent three of their planning department staff to appraise this monstrous invasion of the council rules and by-laws. Raymond was worried about this invasion, and expected, quite naturally, to be closed down. He thought a petition by all of his customers might win the day, if it was necessary.

On the day of the visit by the council staff, two of whom turned out to be regular customers, the sun was shining and world was at peace. The council staff checked out the structure for stability and safety and could find no faults there. The situation was getting sticky until Raymond pointed out that the van was not a fixed building. He showed them that it had wheels with all the tyres inflated and ready for the road. The lights and the flashers were working according to rules, as were the hydraulic brakes, and Raymond had obtained a certificate of roadworthiness from a friend in the transport department. He told the council staff that all he needed to drive the van around was a replacement engine, which was proving hard to find, and when he did, he meant to apply for a hawker's licence to make it fully mobile. For the time being though they asked him where he was sourcing his produce, so he took them for a tour of inspection. They told him that he could quite legally sell any goods produced on his own property, and they could see that, in fact, that was the case. The only problem of concern was the mushrooms which they believed he bought in from suppliers elsewhere. Oh boy, were they amazed when he took them for a tour of the mushroom cellars, and Raymond tested them out when he asked, "What about my honey sales. I have no control on where the bees source the nectar. as they travel a long distance when foraging. He had six hives at home in the garden, and offered to open them up so they could see his bees at work. but they vetoed the offer, although one lady was keen to inspect the hives for her own amusement, Raymond offered to allow that lady to attend next time the hives were ready for harvesting, and promised to ring her office a few days before hand. He explained that he had plenty of spare protective clothing which she could borrow. They did not realise, that much of Raymond's stock was actually brought in. He could sell that produce whenever he had a tree or garden patch, to produce them on site, and once harvested no-one knew where they were grown.

Ray was having some difficulty keeping his Granny and Ma Osbourne from over working themselves. They were both elderly and somewhat disabled and he insisted that they rest on the chairs that he had placed in the van whenever possible. They were both a stubborn as mules. It was very good to have either one or the other as stand by shop assistants when he had to dash off somewhere, or attend to one of the many events that regularly cropped up, and they both loved the experience, but now that the business was thriving and younger staff available, and affordable, Ray wanted the oldies

177

to slow down. Every section of the operation, the vegetables, fruit, egg production, and bee keeping, along with the mushroom production, had all turned out to be winners.

So long as the council and the EEC kept out of his way, except for quick routine checks, mainly to enjoy a decent cup of tea, or coffee, and some of the lady's home-made cakes. Ray was coping with jockeying the girls around in his life without getting too close to either of them but it was inevitable that he would need the love and comfort of one or other in the long term, but which one. Purely by chance Melanie stepped up and filled the gap, temporarily.

Ray was turned eighteen by then and both girls were seventeen when Granny Clarke began to fade quite badly. Since Xmas/New Year holiday the weather had been bitterly cold, with frequent frosts and a couple of heavy snow falls. Both old ladies had been house bound most of the time, and both were looking very tired. Granny Clarke succumbed to a very severe cold which quickly turned into a serious bout of influenza and she was very poorly for a few weeks. Once February arrived the weather did not improve, making the garden and stall much more difficult to manage, as most of the staff succumbed to the vicious flu epidemic. Ray seemed to be indomitable except for plenty of sniffles and sneezes and bouts of coughing. He always kept well enough to hold the fort during the worst of the weather. The vegetable side of the business was slow due to the frost but the eggs, honey and mushrooms seemed to thrive. He was running low on honey as everyone was dosing themselves up with it. The heather honey was well appreciated by all his customers, where-as, the hotel trade had, slackened off, as the visitors stayed away in droves. Melanie appeared to be able to lift herself up to help with the many problems that were a daily event. She was quite domesticated at home and quickly took over running the homes to help Ma and Aunty Libby giving them more time to nurse Granny Clarke.

In the middle of February Granny Clarke took a turn for the worse and needed constant care and nursing. Aunt Libby and cousins Paulette and Kathy attended the dear old girl along with daily visits by the district nurse and regular visits

179

by the family doctor but it was all to no avail. They began to realise that Granny was slowly slipping away, and Raymond thought she had lost the will to fight the disease. He was sitting by her bedside on the seventeenth of February and it was close to midnight when she quietly said, "I'm going home in the morning love."

Raymond did not fully understand the meaning or significance of what she had just said.

He gave her an extra big cuddle and kissed her cheek before telling her that this was her home and had been for a number of years. Granny slipped off into a restless sleep that she would never awake from. When his Aunty Libby entered the room it was almost daybreak, and she was surprised to see Raymond still sitting by the bedside. She was about to make some comment, as she lay the tea tray on the dresser, when Raymond stood up quickly, took a few quick steps towards her saying, "She's gone Aunty." He threw his arms around her, hugging her close as they wept quietly.

When he settled down, he told his Aunty what Granny had said about going home. He said to

Aunty, "She knew she was dying and was going home to Grandad and her God in heaven. Do you realise the significance of, 'Yesterday?'" It would have been Grandad's birthday, and I am sure she held on to see it out."

"Oh, heck Raymond, I believe you're right, and she knows we'll inter her remains next to the others in Clifford. What shall we do now, Love?"

"If you can see to the kids, I'll ring the doctor, the undertaker and Father O'Malley. I thought maybe we should shut up shop for the day but she would not want us to do that, so I'll arrange with Margaret and Jenifer to hold the fort and we'll close up altogether on the day of the funeral. That will give us a few days to let the regulars know what's going on and they will have to rearrange their schedules to suit. As soon as I know the details, I'll post a notice on the stall and in the papers. I think we can hold the wake here in the big barn. I'll get one of our best catering customers to organise the food and drinks, and we have plenty of furniture that we used for the socials, Aunty. I'll try to contact 'Shines Amusement Caterers' in Hull city. They had a great affection for your mother, and she for them, so seeing as it's their offseason they might just feel inclined to attend her funeral."

Raymond picked up the telephone and set about making all the arrangements. Their doctor told him there would be no need for a post mortem or inquest because he and the district nurse had been in attendance for many days before hand. He would write out the death certificate and arrange to have his Granny moved to the funeral home at the undertakers in Braham during the day, and leave the arrangements in their hands. One of his restaurants was keen to cater for Granny Clarke because they had so many dealings with her and Raymond. The owner Ronald White, arrived mid-afternoon and checked out the facilities in the barn so they knew what extras would be needed. Then they asked the big question, "Did he have any idea how many to cater for?"

Of course, the answer was: "Who knows? Because of her involvement with the stall, she knew so many people who loved her dearly". He suggested a walk-through smorgasbord arrangement so her friends can come and go as they pleased. He estimated that they would need to cater for at least 50 mourners and maybe more. The restaurant manager said it was much easier to cater like that and they could have plenty in reserve. They would provide roast meats, hams, cheeses, and quickly make them up into extra sandwiches if needed. They would bake a number of large cakes that could be sliced if and when needed. So that was a number of problems taken care of and all it needed now was a large mug of tea to settle his stomach.

The next call would have to be to the amusement caterers in Hull. Raymond spoke to the booking clerk who was very sympathetic. She said that she did not travel with the fairground these days but remembered Sister Charlotte, as she was known in the trade and was happy to pass on the message. During the next couple of days, a number of sympathy cards arrived mainly from the "babies" that she had delivered, and of course their mothers.

The funeral for Granny Clarke was to be held in Clifford church, and the interment to follow

next to the rest of Raymond's family. A grave
site had been set aside between his father's
grave and his Grandfather's grave ready to
accept the old lady. A couple of coaches had
been hired to ferry any mourners who needed
transport from Leeds to Clifford and back
again, enabling them to attend. Raymond, Aunt
Libby, and family, were the last to leave the
church, for the wake, after they had thanked
the convent sisters, who had to get back to
their classrooms. A number of lay-sisters and
some mothers had been called in to hold the
fort, so the teaching sisters, who were familiar
with Sister Charlotte, could attend the funeral
mass and internment. When the family arrive
back at the farm the scene was pure bedlam.
The farm yard, and Metcalf's yard, were full and
overflowing, and the road outside lined with
parked cars. The caterers were flat out serving
food and drinks. A small bar had been set up
in one corner to dispense alcoholic beverages,
such as port and sherry, for those who enjoyed
that sort of drink. Raymond had set up his
Radiogram and a pile of Granny's favourite
music, hymns as well as old time favourites,

and this was providing fun and entertainment for all. The party was due to run on until very late, although the strong drinks ran out early and the food a little later. The older members of the crowd began to disperse once they were replete but the younger members continued to dance the night away. It was nearly midnight by the time the barn was cleared, and Raymond closed the big wooden doors He was totally exhausted, as were his cousins and some of his staff. After a couple of days to let it all sink in, Raymond called at the other house to have a chat with his Aunty. He told her that Grandma Clarke never had much in the way of assets, but in recent years she had at last managed to amass a sizable estate, thanks to the garden and shop. Her Prudential life assurance, which had run for many years, had yielded quite a good deal of cash. Since she had been living with Mrs. Osbourne she had saved a deal of money from her old aged pension, because, both she and uncle Fred had been told to keep their rent money. Ma reckoned they both worked for more than the rent as worth. The market garden, and stall, provided for all their utilities and food, except for meat. "Putting all this together, Aunt Libby, you will receive a tidy sum of money which I intend to deposit in your name. I don't need any of it, and I want you to have it to repay you for all the love and care you loaded on Gran and me over many years. Maybe you might want to give some of it away to your kids, that's up to you, but it is all yours, to do with as you please. You and Uncle Fred have worked very hard and scored well in spite of Uncles deafness. Go and take a decent holiday with the kids. Let your hair down and see how you go. We can manage here without you, although we will miss you all, both personally and in the business." Aunty Libby grabbed a firm hold of him and squeezed like mad with tears pouring down her cheeks, then said, 'Oh Raymond, you can't do this, it's not right. The money should go to you, after all it was your hard work and dedication that earned it."

Ray finally let her go and stepped back a little from her but kept hold of both her hands, then looking right into her eyes reiterated, "No Aunty, I will have no argument about this. You still have three young children to bring up and educate and you will need all this, and maybe more, to make sure they get the best chances in life. Please take it and spend it wisely, and thanks for your support through all my trials and tribulations." She pulled him into her arms again expressing her gratitude for his generosity.

Chapter Seven

Another Sad Day

It was only a short time later, seven months to be precise, that Raymond entered Ma Osbourne's bedroom at the crack of dawn with her usual tray of tea and toast. She was very still in the big double bed and didn't sit up to greet him as he entered. He put the tray down on the bedside table and approached the bed, then lay a hand on her shoulder but she never moved. He checked her pulse but there was no sign of life. He checked for other signs of life before realising that the old lady had passed away quietly during the night. She had been warned about the sorry condition of her heart, even before Raymond entered her life, and it was nothing short of a miracle that she had survived this long. He covered her face with the sheet and left the room. He was so sure that the old lady was in fact deceased, that he didn't bother to call the doctor until a more social hour. Later, when he picked up the telephone extension from the office table and called the doctor, he was not at all surprised. He called in on his daily rounds and issued the death certificate.

As with his Grandmother earlier in the year. Ray was faced with making all the preparations for the funeral and wake. His Granny's wake was such a great success that he quite naturally decided to repeat the event in a similar mode. However; this time there would be many more complications. Everything; the houses, the farm, the business etc, were all in Ma Osbourne's name, as far as he knew anyway, which meant that he and the rest of the family would most likely have to find other accommodation, and remove the stall [van] to other premises. Raymond himself would be as well set up, also the Van, by moving across the road to the Metcalf property. He knew he would be welcomed over there as they had discussed the possibility of council forcing him to move the Van. His Aunt Libby was a different proposition, with four children under foot, she would need a large house to fit them all in. He did not have any idea where he stood with Mrs. Osbourne's estate because she had never discussed her situation with him, other than when he first arrived and moved into her home. At that time, she told him, and his Granny that she was all alone now that her only son and grandson had gone and there were no other relatives at all.

In a mode of panic, after all everything he now owned, was tied up with Mrs. Osbourne's estate. All his crops, machinery, and other infrastructure, were attached to her property. Nothing at all was in his name. Presumably, the whole property and houses, would be put up for sale, leaving them all destitute. He took out his key for Ma's safe, which was hidden in her office wall and opened it up. He had often done that but only to take out the cash float and sometimes obtain change for the till. He had no idea what else it might contain. There were insurance policies on the shelf, a quantity of legal documents relating to the lease of her farm land and other matters, but there was no will. He checked the separate locked drawer at the bottom, finding only a copy of the title deeds to the farm but little else. One important item he did find, were the details of a firm of solicitors who appeared to handle all her business.

His aunt Libby came in and put the kettle on the Aga stove to make them morning teas, before she realised that Raymond was very quiet and seemed to be distressed. She asked him, "Are you alright our Raymond? You look shocked. Has something else happened? Whatever is the matter love?"

He said, "It's Mrs. Osbourne, Aunty. I took her morning tea in to her and she was gone, deceased. She had passed away in her sleep. Her sick old heart must have finally given up the ghost."

Aunt Libby put her arms around him and hugged him tightly asking him, "What are you going to do, love? You'll have to arrange for the doctor to come around, then, arrange her funeral, won't you?"

"Yes, all that and a lot more aunty. I believe everything is in her name, and I don't know where to go or what to do. I can move across the road and set the stall up in Metcalf's driveway, and live with them for now. I had a look in the safe but there is no will in there, nor any other instructions, other than I found the details of a firm of solicitors that she used. I was just about to telephone their office to see if I can get an early appointment to talk to one of the partners. A Mr. Wilkinson seems to have dealt with all her business, so I'll see if he can help me. Have you got the kettle on, I need a pot of tea and some breakfast before I call the solicitor's office. I have already rung the doctor's surgery and he'll call in on his rounds. I've got the solicitor's phone number so I'll ring them shortly, and this Wilkinson bloke might have some answers." Without more ado he picked up the phone and spoke to the receptionist at the solicitors, and told her about Mrs. Osbourne's passing away, and asking for an urgent appointment with Mr. Wilkinson. She replied "Mr. Wilkinson has a few minutes now, and I am sure he'd want to know because he was very fond of Mrs. Osbourne. Please hold the line I'll transfer you now."

After introductions, Mr. Wilkinson asked, "What happened to my dear old friend, Raymond, you say she has passed away."

"Yes sir, I took her tea in early this morning and I got no response, so I checked her pulse and other vital statistics and I got the impression she had passed away earlier in the night as her hand was quite cool. I've called her doctor and he's due soon."

"Ok then Raymond, I need to see you urgently to let you know how you stand with all this. Don't worry yourself about a thing until we have a chat, shall we say 3.00pm. this afternoon. Would that fit in with your plans? As I said, you and your aunty have nothing to worry about. Mrs. Osbourne has provided for you both and I will explain all that when you get here this afternoon. I'll see you then, ok."

"Yes, thank you Mr. Wilkinson, that's somewhat of a relief already, you seem to be many steps ahead of me. Thank you very much sir, good bye for now." and he hung up the phone before turning to his aunty with a bit of a smile on his face. "Good news Aunty, it seems that Ma left some instructions with her solicitor, just in case her heart did give up suddenly."

At the appointed time, Raymond arrived at the solicitor's office and was shown into

Mr. Wilkinson's private office, where he was invited to sit down. The secretary, Rosalind, followed him in with a tray of tea and coffee as well as cake and biscuits. After serving the tea, she took a seat at the end of the huge desk and with pen and pad in hand prepared to write down minutes of the meeting.

Mr Wilkinson began with, "Well Raymond, this is indeed a sad day for all of us, although we are amazed that Mrs. Osbourne lived this long. The doctors had her written off long before you even met her, and I honestly believe, that meeting and getting to know you, prolonged her life until today. She thought the world of you. She admired you, and all that you've achieved. You filled a large hole in her life after losing her family, just as I believe you did with yours. Did you bring proof of your identity with you, and her death certificate?"

"Yes, Sir I did. This is my birth certificate issued in Kent." Raymond handed it over to him who, after perusing the details passed it over to his secretary, who was to copy it and file the copy.

Mr. Wilkinson then remarked, "As of today Raymond you are a very rich young man.

Mrs. Osbourne left you her entire estate and assets which are very extensive, not just the farm. Because she lived beyond the statutory time after her bequest to you, all taxes and charges have been wavered. No gift duty is applicable, but there may be other taxes payable. The estate will have to go before probate, but much of her wealth was gifted to you at the beginning of your acquaintance, so is clear of death duties, and probate also. She kept all this secret from you so no-one can claim collusion. The farm and all her other assets have been yours all this time. Only Rosalind here, and myself were aware of these transfers. From today the returns from the farm lease agreement will be paid directly into your account, and we will both need to see your bank manager and accountant to streamline everything. I believe that you also bank at the same branch as Mrs. Osbourne, and use the same accountant, Alex Littlewood, which will make any transition easy for you. Now to continue, there are in existence a number of deposit boxes, containing a good deal of valuable objects, that even I have no knowledge of but they are also vested in your name not hers. You can excise any or all of that property at any time. I suggest you take the time now, open those boxes and catalogue all the contents carefully so I can advise you of which to keep and which to dispose of. A good deal of the property will need to be professionally valued, and there are, I believe a certain amount of deeds of title and ownership that I will need to catalogue. I have decided to allocate the services of my secretary, Rosalind here, to go with you now to the bank, and assess all your property and wealth. She will know how to best catalogue each item.

I would love to accompany you myself but I have other clients. It will be like opening Pandora's box. So that's it for now, go along with Rosalind, who I believe has made the necessary arrangements with the bank manager, Mr Jameson, and Raymond, Good Luck. I believe you have never needed a solicitor before today but I hope you will bless our firm with your business in the future. I will pledge my good name to assure you that you will receive the best of our attention."

"Well, you leave me little choice, Mr. Wilkinson. You have been very kind and very astute in attending to what was in fact my estate. I suppose, reading between the lines of course, that you are now in a position to send me huge bills for past services as well as the future ones."

"No, no, Raymond everything is paid up to date, so we can start from this moment onwards, thank you. Anyway, you're going to need to find some way to spend all your money, and you will need lots of tax deductions from now on, so keep in contact with me and our acquaintance Alex Littlewood." Just one further point I should have you consider, although you are still quite young, I would be remiss in my duties if I failed to suggest you make an appointment with myself, or another solicitor of your choice, and make out a carefully worded 'Last Will and Testament.' They shook hands warmly and firmly as he and Rosalind stepped out of the office together.

A small office was made available for Rosalind and Raymond at the nearby bank and they began with box number one. Raymond was a little disappointed when it was full of papers, but he cheered up when Rosalind explained what they actually were. The box contained a quantity of deeds, share certificates and other valuable documents, which Rosalind catalogued for valuation. Raymond asked her, "How come there is such a wealth of assets in here. Surely the old lady couldn't amass this much from farming."

Rosalind explained that very little of it was derived from farming. She explained that Mr. Osbourne had left a sizable life assurance when he died, and his wife invested most of it in stocks and shares. Then, when her son was killed, he had held a very sizable life assurance, and the airline had to pay out a huge amount of compensation due because of his and his son's death. Then to cap it all off she had insured her grandson with a life assurance policy, added to the travel insurance and airline compensation. She did not need any of it to live on because she had the lease money from the farm and some income from the garden and orchard which she sold from the roadside stall. The second box was stacked with bank notes which Rosalind counted and recorded. Box number three was full of top, quality jewellery, some of which were family heirlooms and others bought with the life assurances. Rosalind told him that all this wealth was quite useful, but it had failed to fill her direst needs. She was a wealthy woman without a family of any sort, hence she latched onto Raymond with a passion. Fortunately, he came to the party and loved her back with all his might. They were two of a kind and desperately needed one another, and each fulfilled that need. The fourth box was filled with more deeds and share certificates meaning lots more work for Rosalind. Rosalind then called in the bank manager to round off the rest of the estate. He pointed out to them, that Mrs. Osbourne was living comfortably before Ray came on the scene and since then she had amassed a good deal of cash which he believed was remittances from the revised stall income, as well as dividends from her many stocks and shares. All this meant that her current account was very substantial as well. Jokingly, Raymond stated, "I suppose that means she can well afford to pay for her own funeral as well."

"Oh no Raymond, Mrs. Osbourne has already paid for her own funeral a good few years ago, knowing that she had a bad heart. Mr Wilkinson will have all the details of that affair, the church details, wake etc."

After recording all the contents of the boxes, they asked for all the documents relating to the bank accounts held in her name. There was a general trading account heavily in credit, a modest savings account, and a special savings account ready for the taxman. Raymond was absolutely floored. This was all too much to take in on one go. He now owned two large farm houses, a decent acreage of good grazing land, stocks, shares, jewellery, and heaps of ready cash. He was going to need to be very astute, never-the-less, to make sure that not one penny of it was wasted. His old car would have to go and be replaced with a modest vehicle useful for work as well as social outings. The work part indicated a large diesel panel van of some sort which might double as a family car, or maybe he could buy two vehicles; a nice cheap sedan and a large van.

"Ok Rosalind, you have all you need to get started, and I have heaps to attend to before this day is over. Thank you so much for your time and patience. Would you be kind enough to arrange a suitable appointment with Mr. Wilkinson, to sort out the business of a will, please. Good afternoon."

"Yes of course Raymond, leave it with me and I will give you a call quite soon. Thank you, Raymond, and Good afternoon."

Raymond returned home to catch up with the family. He was able to tell his Aunty, Uncle and the kids that they could relax and enjoy their family home. Over a large pot of tea, he explained a little of what had occurred at the solicitor's office and also at the bank. He only told his Aunty that he had inherited both houses, and the land surrounding them. The garden, orchards and farm buildings, were included in the deal. He was very careful not to mention the contents of the safety deposit boxes. His Aunt was astounded, and they shared a good deal of cuddles and tears, which eventually helped to calm them down.

Aunty Libby quickly got to grips with the new scenario and said, "Does that mean we'll have to pay the rent for our house to you instead of Mrs. Osbourne, our Raymond.

He replied, "That's up to you and Uncle Fred, Aunty. I still need you as back-up to run the stall, and I still need Uncle Fred to look after the buildings as he has been doing in the past. I believe that will amply reward me for supplying free accommodation for you all, and free fruit and vegetables, should leave you ahead of the game. Have a talk about it amongst yourselves and let me know how you feel about it. It's early days yet and we have a funeral to organise.

The funeral of Ma Osbourne would not be an epic event. As she had no family, the mourners were mainly customers and local people. The church service was well attended, and the church was a mass of flowers. The stall was closed for the whole day, and the wake was held as before in the big barn. Although there were not as many as were gathered for his Granny's funeral the food was top notch and the dancing went on almost to midnight. Ma was of Anglican faith but that changed very little, and a good time was had by all. By the time all the funeral business was out of the way, and Ray had time to sit down and think about his life, he realised that once again his "Family," had been stolen away from him. Admittedly, he still had his Aunty and Uncle with their four kids in tow. They were a good family together, fortunately, but Raymond was totally bereft of real emotions. His best option for the future was long hours of work, and very satisfying labours to fill the gaps.

Once the funeral was out of the way. Ray decided to rearrange the vehicles at his disposal. He transferred Mrs Osbourne's A40 estate car into Paulette's name so they would feel free to use it when they felt like it. Paulette was glad to have use of a car that she felt was her own, so she could ferry the family around. Her mother had never learned to drive, but her father had a current licence to drive, as did Paulette.

Ray drove his own Austin car to the nearest dealer, the local Ford dealer as it turned out, and organised to purchase a heavy-duty ford Thames panel van with a high roof, diesel engine and a good solid towing bar, mainly for the bee hives and honey transport. Ray drove the van around to the college to show his tutor, Mr. Robertson. They decided to build a strong gantry to fit in the van with a slide out arm and a heavy hook attached. Ray owned a neat chain hoist that would hook onto the gantry to hoist the hives up and slide them inside. The special set of forks made for the trailer would hook on the hoist of the van and fit under the hives.

He bought a near new Ford Zephyr for his own use, and it was also equipped with a heavy-duty towing bar to move the hives around. The six-cylinder engine would be useful for that job and others. He also purchased a tandem axle box trailer to work behind either of the new vehicles, to carry any unsavoury goods such as farm manures and compost and awkward goods like building materials and garden machinery. It would be a big load for the Zephyr, but when Ray measured the trailer, he realised that the Ferguson tractor would fit on to it, provided he was careful. The trailer was fitted with over run brakes which would be handy at least, and he designed and built a strong canopy to bolt onto the side rails.

A couple of days after the funeral he realised that he needed to start robbing the hives. Some of them must be full to bursting by now, so he loaded some of the new boxes and frames into the Thames van ready to leave early the next morning. Melanie arrived early so he took her along with him. The hives were deep into the moorland where he had located a nice wide gully with a small trickle of a stream running through it. The gully protected the hives from high winds and the bees needed a supply of water, however, the access was difficult and needed extreme care. They turned off the main road about twenty miles or so from home onto a steep, dirt road, which soon became a farm track, before deteriorating along a rough access way with grass and bushes brushing alongside his lovely new van. Melanie was quite perturbed, and wondered if they would ever get back onto the road again. She relaxed once she saw the lovely sward of grassland alongside the stream with the hives nestled under the overhang of the embankment.

They unloaded the equipment from the van and lit the smoker. Once the smoker was going well and they were dressed for the fray, they pitched in with a will. The queen excluders had worked well making the job so much easier. He opened the first of the ten hives and was surprised how heavy they were. He removed each frame one by one and replaced it with a new empty one. The full frames fitted into the spare boxes which were sitting in zinc trays to catch any spillage. The van soon had a good load on board and the hives were working again already. Melanie was amazed at how quickly the bees returned to their job. As they were packing up their equipment he looked up and spotted a horse and rider approaching. Even from a distance he could see that the rider was female and the horse was serious quality, well-bred and well groomed.

The young lady riding the horse seemed to be quite aggressive, and unwelcoming, despite his best endeavours to be friendly. She snapped at him, "Who the hell are you two, and what are you doing here? If you think you can steal those hives and the honey you can think again. I'll record the make, model, and registration of your vehicle and report you to the police."

"Well, well, well, a rude, ignorant, native of the species. What right have you to question us? You're not a copper nor even a warden of some sort, so pull your head in, madam."

"There is no need to take that attitude because I know those hives, they belong to a Lady who drives a blue A70 motor car. I don't know her by name but she has been bringing hives up onto this moor for years, although I have never seen them in this gully before."

"Ok madam, the lady's name is Mrs Featherstone, and I have bought her out. All this is mine now. Here, this is the lady's phone number, so give her a call when you get home."

So saying, Ray took out his note book and wrote down a telephone number and passed it to her. Asking "Anyway, who the heck "are," you, and what right do you have to question me? Where have you come from? We haven't seen any homesteads for many miles around here."

The woman replied, "My family live over in the next valley just behind that high knob yonder. This track skirts around the base of the knob, then it cuts across the ridge, and enters the next valley. I ride through here every day, and sometimes twice a day. I'll check your details when I get home before I report you to the police." Ray remembered that he had put some of his business cards in the glove box of the van. He went to retrieve one of them gave it to the woman, girl actually, along with a jar of honey from the van then told her to bugger off because he had work to do. She was still mouthing obscenities at him as they drove away.

He carefully manoeuvred the van along the moorland track, out on to the tarmac road and headed for home. Actually, this load was going straight to Mrs Featherstone's extraction and bottling rooms. She was totally dumb struck when she tested the weight of the frames, then she said, "There you are young man, what did I tell you about moving and positioning the hives to maximise production? Which of my sites did you use?"

"The point is Mabel I didn't use any of your sites. I found an ideal sheltered gully with a trickle of a stream running in the bottom and plenty of grass alongside. The road in is a nightmare, but the Thames van coped fairly well, just that it was very slow going, especially on the return trip. I didn't want all the honey to decant over the bumps" He explained where he had found the gully, and Mabel admitted that she had looked at the site in the past but reckoned it was far too difficult, for either her or her A70 to access safely. She said the next valley had much better access because there was a homestead higher up under the crag close to the summit. She placed her hives on the lower end where there was a nice flat grassy area and reasonably good access.

They quickly unloaded the boxes full of honey, and Melanie stayed with the old lady to help her uncap the frames, extract the honey, and bottle some of it. Ray said, "I'll collect you at about 5pm, Melanie, have a good day. See you later Mabel, please don't rush yourself I still have a few jars left. I'll take a load of bottled honey back with me tonight if you have any ready. Do you have plenty of heather honey labels or do I need to order more?"

"Thanks Ray, I have a hundred or so on hand but I'll ring the printer now and order 500 more, Thanks for all this and I'll see you tonight, bye."

As the weather began to close in prior to winter, Ray had to arrange a day to collect the rest of the moorland hives and bring them home for the winter. The weather had remained sunny meaning the hives would be heavy again. He would need to make two trips or risk overloading the van. Adding the trailer would be ok on decent roads but not up in the moorland tracks. It was on the second trip that he got a surprise. As he approached the line of hives, the girl with the horse rode towards him. She slid off the horse nearby but safely away from possible stings, she hoped. Anyway, she tethered her to a small bush. Raymond carried on with loading the hives and the girl called out to him. "Can I come and talk to you, Mister Clarke?"

"You stay back there because there are still lots of angry bees around. I'll come over to you."

She began with, "Hi I'm Mandy Oliver, and I need to sincerely apologise for my rudeness the last time we met. I should have checked your credentials before charging in and attacking you like that. Even then I had no right to suspect you of a serious crime without checking the facts. As I told you before, I live at the other side of that big knob. My Mum and Dad would like to talk to you about placing some hives in our valley next spring. Our road is much better than this one although much longer. Would you have time to call on them, probably today?"

"Ok, seeing as I am nearby, I might as well do that. Where is your place and how do I get there?"

"I'll cut across the moor and meet you in our road. It turns off about 2 miles further along the dirt road. I'll see you there in about half an hour or so, if that's ok."

"I have made a start at packing up here, but about an hour would be better." He turned away back to the van and continued to load the last five bee-hives. Loading was relatively easy now with the overhead gantry. He tidied up the site ready for next time. After carefully negotiating the rough track he easily found the road into the next valley, which was much wider and flatter at the lower end but he could see that it quickly climbed upwards, all the way up to a sharp bend, then disappeared over a ridge. The surface was quite good, apart from a few potholes, as he followed Mandy and her horse. The road eventually wound around into a sort of court-yard behind a stone cottage, then swung out and round a useful barn and other stone sheds and outbuildings, some of which contained a number of pigs due to the noise and aroma.

Mr. and Mrs. Oliver came out of the barn, and Mandy introduced them to Raymond. Mrs. Oliver suggested that they all go into the cottage for refreshments since it was almost lunch time, so they could talk about bees. She told Ray that they were all allergic to bee stings so could not have a hive or two of their own, but if he could find a site nearby it would help them immensely. She said that she had established a kitchen garden behind the barns where the soil was rich and fertile. She had planted a number of fruit trees, which were growing well, as were beans and peas and other plants. However; the flowering vegetables and fruit trees never set much fruit. She believed that they were short of bees, and other insects early in the spring and summer. She told him about Mabel and her hives lower down the valley, but said she only brought them up mid to late summer for the heather honey, so could he help her early in the summer, or better still, early spring. Ray told them that he had had a good summer, not only with the honey flow, but also with the number of swarms of bees out of the hives. He told them that his friends at the trade college had worked extra well and produced a good many new hives and frames to go in them. Instead of losing the swarming bees escaping into nature, he had been able to place the new hives close enough to the existing ones and some of the swarms had taken up residence in them. He'd gained 17 new hives over the summer months so had a surplus, over and above his expected usage for next year. That meant he could supply their place with enough hives to pollinate the farm.

Ray opined that he had seen a limestone crag on the way in that faced southwards towards the sun, offering shelter and reflected heat from the face of the crag. If he could get his van in close to the crag, he might be able to help. After enjoying a delightful early lunch party, they went for a walk. Mr Oliver led them around through a gap between the barn and pig sheds out onto a reasonably level piece of ground ending beneath the crag. Ray marked out a rectangular area which seemed suitable. He placed four large white stones to mark out the site, then said, "Can you keep this area clear of bushes and scrub. You don't need to worry about grass and weeds, then I can access it easily. There's enough room to manoeuvre my van in and out, and that's all I need. There's plenty of water nearby, and this site should stay quite warm. Ok. You, will have to telephone me as soon as you see the buds beginning to open on the plum trees. Don't leave it too late, don't wait to see the open flowers. Down our way the trees begin to flower much earlier than up here, so the bees will be flat out harvesting nectar, and I'll know when to expect your call. You can always leave a message if I am not around, but if you ring after dark I will be around. Right you are then, I'm away. Thank you for the meal and I'll hear from you in the spring, goodbye for now. The Oliver family thanked him profusely and bade him goodbye.

Chapter Eight

Mother and Baby

Both of his own farm yards were soon cluttered with hives over wintering, and preparing for next spring. The bees would need feeding throughout the cold months but he had left a decent supply of honey in each one. The lower boxes which contained the brood combs automatically contained a fair quantity of stored honey but would need supplementing as winter progressed. He now owned 57 active hives and hoped for a large increase as soon as the bees began to swarm. When the weather showed signs of spring, Ray began ferrying out the hives to where best to service the local orchards, and early clover crops. He also placed spare new hives nearby each site, hoping to capture stray swarms as soon as the weather warmed up. He had 6 of the new well stocked hives set up ready for a trip out onto the moors, and he would move out early one morning, when the call was about due. The chances were, that they would not produce as well as those left behind, but a certain lack of competition up there might make the difference between the two sites.

He decided not to wait for a call and set off in the dark the next morning. The Oliver family were happy to see him, and he went straight through to the chosen site, unloaded the hives and opened them up. The bees crawled out into bright sunlight and began foraging for flowers immediately, mainly weeds as yet. As he moved out into the farm yard Mrs. Oliver called out to him to go inside the house for breakfast. There was no sign Mandy as a full farmhouse breakfast was served. on the scrubbed pine table. Ray was surprised that she was absent and raised a query, asking if she was ill or away from home. He had been led to believe that she was an early riser, prior to riding out on the moor on her horse. Ray was surprised when the door burst open and Mandy rushed in asking, "Mum, have you heard from the vet yet. I'm very concerned for Bella. She should have foaled long ago, and she's in great pain. I rang the vet first thing. He should have been here by now. I look like losing both filly and foal if he doesn't get here soon. I've had a good feel around and I can't make any sense of it. There are no legs, nor is there a head. She has been in labour most of the night and can't stand much more. Mum can you please ring the vet and tell him to hurry up. She has collapsed, and has been lying on her side much too long and her lungs will fill with fluids and drown her. Oh! Hello Ray, nice to see you."

"Okay darling, do you want anything to eat?" replied Mrs. Oliver as she hurried into the hall to the telephone. When she returned, she said the vet had gone out on another call, to Major Hollingsworth at the manor house, and was not expected back soon. "Oh! Mum what am I going to do now. I can't lose them both?

Ray said, "Would you like me to have a look, Mandy. I have small hands and have delivered pigs, lambs and calves in the past?"

Mandy replied with a desperate quail, "Oh yes please do, come over now, I need some help desperately. Oh; you haven't finished eating your breakfast."

"No worry love, I'll follow, you lead the way. Have you got hot water, disinfectant and soap?"

"Yes, got all that. I only need to switch the electric kettle back on, so come on, hurry up, get cracking or it will be too late, if it's not already."

They both trotted out to the stables and Mr Oliver followed on behind, although freely admitting that he would be useless, especially if there was any blood about.

Raymond was tearing off his outer clothing as they ran across the yard, and into the stable, where it was a little warmer. The filly was lying on her side and trying to strain against the foal. Raymond quickly slipped his hand up into the birth canal, and was glad to realise there was lots of room for him to reach in, but like Mandy said, there was nothing sticking out to get hold of. He was groping around feeling for legs, at least, or maybe a head, when the filly suffered a massive contraction and nearly chopped his arm off. Pigs and sheep were painful but this was agony. He asked Mandy to cuddle the filly's head and talk quietly to her to try and reassure her, and stop her straining, if she could.

Oh my god he thought, there must be some legs in here somewhere, but where? Realising that Bella had been lying on her side for too long, he called out to Mr. Oliver, "Have you got a pulley block or some other lifting tackle? We need to get Bella up onto her chest, at least. We also need a leather belly band, like they used to use for ploughing if you have one."

"Yeah ok, I have all that in the workshop, so come on Mandy help me carry it. We'll need the step ladder as well, so hurry yourself up lass."

When they returned Ray pointed up to a large ring set in the roof beam and told them to hook the pulley up there, then see-saw the plough harness under the filly's head and neck and try to get it below her shoulder blade, then hook the two ends together and through the hook on the pulley block. He pointed out that there was a tethering ring set into the wall nearby and to hitch the free end of the rope onto, and take a turn around the ring to steady the rope.

Meanwhile, Ray carried on working his way around the foal. He stretched right up along what appeared the be a flank, but which side, when the filly suddenly relaxed a little and he could reach a bit further and realising his hand was holding what felt like a lower rib bone, or so he hoped. The position of the rib bone told him that the head end was to his righthand side, meaning the foal had to move rearwards to his left, and rotate towards him. His arm felt like someone was cutting it off but there was some movement. The filly obviously felt the foal move, and folded her great body up, and followed with a massive contraction, as she was hauled up onto her chest by the rope. Raymond screamed out loudly, and swore profusely, as the pain hit hard. However, the combined effort of filly and the young man were enough to start things off again. Soon he managed to get hold of one leg, which was fortunately bent double at the knee, and pull it round towards him. Next, he stretched in deeper, and hooked his fingers into the nostrils, and pulled hard to get the head around. That's when he realised, he was dealing with a live foal, and as it kicked and snorted, it rolled over on its side allowing the head to move round and down into the birth canal. He was then able to pull the other leg around alongside the head. He called out for the calving ropes, which Amanda had placed nearby, and lassoed them onto each little hoof. Amanda could now pull the feet down firmly into the canal, seesawing them, rather than just pulling both together, as Raymond worked on the head. Soon all the drama was over as the foal slid down onto the straw. Amanda rubbed the foal all over with handfuls of straw ready for Mum to lick him clean. The filly was snorting and sneezing as she tried to clear her lungs and airways. They carried the foal between them and laid her near her mum's nose. The foal was a filly which delighted Amanda and her dad. At that moment Mrs. Oliver appeared in the stable doorway, calling out before entering to let them know she was there, and bearing a welcome tray of refreshments. Ray was massaging his sore arm trying to get the circulation going again, and washing the blood and gore off it.

As the drama was subsiding, Ray was surprised when Amanda suddenly grabbed hold of him and kissed him soundly, then began to thank him for his help. She said he should have been a veterinary surgeon not a bee keeper. Ray replied, "All that drama was just physical strain and stamina. You only need to be strong and stupid to stick your arm into the birth canal of a horse when she is foaling. There's no need to go to university to learn that. Oh, by the way, sorry for my language earlier. The pain was so intense I couldn't help it."

Amanda replied, "Oh don't worry about that, I hear worse at school. The main thing is, that you got her out alive, and the mother is ok by the looks of it."

The foal quickly got her act together managing the stand wobbly on her feet so she could feed hungrily on her Mum's teats and get a good supply of essential colostrum to set her up for life. This early form of milk is essential, because it's full of antibodies, vitamins, and minerals to ward off infections. Meanwhile, the adults headed for the kitchen, for tea, and toast, and a chat. The Oliver's were delighted with the outcome and showered Ray with thanks and praise. Mr Oliver said, "If Amanda had lost either the foal or her mother, or worse both of them, she would have been devastated, we all would. Thank goodness you managed to prevent that from happening, and if we can ever repay you just ask. Now, how much do we owe you for this morning's effort. The vet would have asked for a huge fee, whether he managed to save both our animals or not?"

Ray replied, "Nothing at all, I was glad to help out, and thank goodness I was here."

"We'll have none of that young man. I'll write you out a substantial cheque to cover your wasted time, because we know how busy you are." Before leaving, Ray looked into the stable again and all was well, with Amanda cuddling the foal and her mum. She jumped to her feet when she saw him, ran to him and delivered another mighty hug and a few juicy kisses. Ray turned to leave as a Range Rover pulled up nearby. The occupant, obviously the errant Vet, extracted himself and opened the rear door to collect his bag of tricks. "Amanda rushed up to him and said, "You won't need your bag of tricks today, in fact, we won't be needing you ever again, so you can bugger off back and see to your posh customers. My foal was delivered safely, thanks to Raymond here, and is now suckling well. You won't be getting any money from us today, and you might remember that next time we need you." The vet went crazy, ranting and raving as he stormed over to the house to see Amanda's parents, but he got short shift from them as well. He threatened to sue Raymond for presuming to act as a vet, when not qualified to do so. Mr Oliver pointed out that anyone can assist a neighbour or friend to alleviate the pain and suffering of an animal and does not need to be a certified professional to do that. The Vet left the farm in a rare old stew, but he could do nothing to change the situation; although he did have the decency to admit he was pleased everything went well in the end. As he said, "A dead horse, and a dead foal, would not be a likely recommendation to any other members of the pony club."

Raymond headed off home at last being well pleased with his morning's work, and the cheque in his pocket, although he was still massaging his sore arm. The outcome was a healthy foal, and a mob of hungry bees, to pollinate the fruit trees in Oliver's orchard and garden. A good morning's work all round. Back at home everything was in turmoil. The stall was very busy and all the staff working like mad. Ray whipped off his jacket and went to work. Firstly, to check out the stall, making a list of any shortages, then heading off to correct the in-balances. There were still crops to harvest, and eggs to collect, before feeding the hens. Next into the green house for a respite from the cold but all was well in there. Next on the list was a trip to see Mabel and stock up with honey. Mabel was delighted with the idea of sending hives out onto the moor even though it was a little early. She made the comment that it would be interesting to see the difference between the home hives, and moorland ones, when the honey was weighed.

It was some weeks later that Ray decided to weigh some of his hives and harvest the current crop of spring flower honey. It had been a very warm mild spring, with nice moderate winds, allowing the bees to work long hours, and the hives were bursting with honey. With so many hives around the district, it took him all week to exchange the frames and get the full ones to Mabel and her crew. He then set aside a Wednesday morning and drove out to the moors to assess the difference between the two sites. He loaded the van with a variety of produce and headed out quite early. Stopping close to the house, he greeted Mrs. Oliver with an arm full of early vegetables and dumped them on the kitchen table, before returning to the van for the rest of the load. Mrs. Oliver was astounded with the quantity and variety of produce, some of which were very early. Then she spied the mushrooms. She asked him, "How on earth did you get mushrooms this early Raymond? We only ever see them in Autumn, after rain." Ray told her about his three cellars full of mushroom beds, with a number of varieties available most of the time.

She got out her purse to pay Raymond for the produce but he told her to put it away again, because, he was not expecting her to pay for the goods, pointing out that much of what he had brought was rejects from the stall. There were bent carrots misshaped cabbages and cauliflowers etc. that he would not display on

227

the stall, but would be prime eating for most people. The kettle was boiling on the AGA stove, so they enjoyed a cup of tea and some fresh toast, with some of his heather honey before he went out to check the hives. He asked, "I suppose Mandy is out riding again."

"Oh yes, but she should be back soon. She never stays away for long now that she has the foal to worry about."

Ray was surprised as he began stripping the hives because they were almost as full as the ones at home, and the honey tasted great. There was only one hive left when Amanda appeared and tethered her horse a safe distance away, before racing forward to embrace Ray. He stopped her before she got too close and reminded her that the air was thick with angry bees. She said, "I would love to see inside the hives, and watch you harvest the honey Raymond."

He replied that he always carried a spare set of protective clothing in the van. He retrieved the special zippered overalls and head wear and they fitted them on her over the top of her riding gear, which was nearly bee proof anyway.

He showed her how to work the smoker, and left her to handle that while he lifted the lid and began removing the frames to the spare box, after brushing off the bees. Soon all was done, and they headed out behind the main barn where there was a sheltered grassy field. The mare and foal were feeding quietly and came to hand easily. Ray pulled a bent carrot from his pocket and fed it to the mare. Whilst keeping a close watch on her foal, she nuzzled up to him hoping for more. Amanda commented, "Well Raymond isn't that the most beautiful foal you have ever seen, and all thanks to you." She put her arm around him and pulled him close for a big hug and a kiss on his cheek.

They eventually got tired of admiring the foal, and walked over to the house, where her Mum went into raptures about all the produce Ray had brought. Ray pulled out one of the frames of honey and asked for a baking tray and a carving knife. He carefully removed all of the honey comb from the frame by cutting it off the wires, and laid it out on the baking tray, as he invited them to taste some of their own honey. After a huge feed of fresh, homemade bread, still warm, from the oven and homemade butter covered with fresh honey comb Mrs. Oliver insisted they all go out into the garden and orchard to check on the work done by the bees. There she pointed out that there was a big crop of peas, and beans, already podding up, and all her fruit trees had set lots of fruit. She was all set for a bumper crop this year. She then showed concern for future years, what would happen then? Ray pointed out that he would leave the hives where they are now, because there were obviously enough flowers around, even this early in the season, and there was yet the heather honey still to come.

Ray needed to scoot out of there, and get back home to his mad house. There was still plenty of daylight left to unload the honey combs at Mabel's place and load up with more bottled honey and some of her pickles and relishes. Mabel was most impressed at the amount of honey, and the excellent flavour, of it and Ray arranged to send a couple of girls around the next morning to sterilise bottles, print labels and stick them in place, as well as help with the extracting, and bottling, of the honey. Saturday morning Melanie fronted up and pitched in with enthusiasm, working mainly with the mushrooms ready for a busy day. Ray placed his arms around her waist and delivered a great big hungry kiss on her lips. When he could speak again, he offered to take her out after work for dinner and a show of some kind. Melanie was speechless for a while then said, "I would need to get back home have a bath, and get Mum to do my hair, so if you could pick me up at home, then I am all yours for the evening. Where will you take me?" Ray gave that some thought and replied, I'll pick the restaurant and you pick the show."

"Oh goody. I would love to go to Leeds City Variety show, if that's ok. All my friends go there and they reckon it's a fabulous show." Ray agreed whole heartedly, and he selected one of his favourite restaurants who always shopped at the stall. The manager and chef were great friends with both Ray and Melanie. He knew that Jenifer would not be happy with his date but he could not take both girls. Jenifer was by now permanently employed and her Mum needed her support whereas Melanie was well

231

supported by a family at home. Ray was so well supported with all the people who worked for him, and with him, that he was astounded. Compared to the lonely life at home in his early days, this was paradise. Most of his customers, both tradesmen and individuals, seemed to respect, and even revere, him due to his endless enthusiasm and pleasant civility. He often mentioned to his staff that a smile and a little civility came free of charge and were worth a great deal of money to them all.

The morning after the night out with Melanie, Ray had a bright idea that might or might not work out. His house and home were enormous, and he had very little time to enjoy it. Meals were always a problem, and he couldn't live on fish and chips all the time. His laundry was becoming a big problem too especially now he appeared to have a social life looming. He asked Margaret and Jenifer to come up to the house during a quiet time and sent Aunty Libby and Paulette to relieve them for an hour or so.

They all went into the house and climbed the stairs to the second floor which hadn't been used for a very long time. Ray escorted them around and into every room. There was a nice bathroom needing a bit of refurbishment, four good sized bedrooms, and a fifth master bedroom. All were overdue for a refurbishment, and some structural changes. The ladies were astounded by the size and number of rooms. Ray asked them, "How would it fit into your lifestyle, if you were to move in here instead of travelling back and forth. Uncle Fred could make the upgrades and create a comfortable kitchen to turn the whole floor into a self-contained flat. He would repaint the whole floor and carry out any repairs. He pointed out some of the many benefits of living on site. No more bus fares. No more waiting about in all weathers for the bus, and trying to fit their schedule into the bus timetables. They would save all the wasted time travelling back and forth to get to work, especially in the winter.

Margaret commented, "You are joking Raymond. If that was possible it would be magic, and we would all benefit, but there must be a snag or two, surely"

"Only one small one. I need a house keeper, to cook for me, and a laundry maid to look after me and my part of the house. I realise that you will need to put in a fair amount of thought before agreeing to any of this, so let me know what you think about my proposal. There would be no more electricity, water, or gas bills, to worry about, and no rent to pay, and no garden to look after."

"Would we be able to use your laundry, washing machine and drier for our stuff as well as for yours?"

"Yes of course and any other appliances like the vacuum cleaner, for example"

"Ok done deal, we don't need to think about any of it. When can we move in?

"I'll talk to Uncle Fred when he gets home. You can always move in any time you're ready and sleep here, using my kitchen and bathroom until yours is ready. Grab the vacuum any time you feel like it and start cleaning your rooms. Any spare furniture, yours or mine can be stored in the attics. There is a trunk full of curtains and some bedding up in the attic, and you can start laundering the existing curtains and anything else as soon as you like."

Jenifer piped up with an idea, saying "Hey Mum, if we get fish and chips for tea we can get started now. We can get one bedroom ready except for painting and do the rest as we go."

Ray said, "As soon as you are ready to eat, I can drive to the Chippy get fish and chips for us all and eat together. There are two spare bedrooms ready to go on my level and plenty of spare linen. That means you can call at your place and grab a few things to see you through until we get time to move your personal things in, whilst Fred gets the painting done."

They drove to Margaret's home and filled the van with many essentials to stock up their new home pending completion of the renovations. After enjoying a fine fish supper together, they unloaded the van and set up the bedrooms for Margaret and Jenifer. Raymond retired to his own part of the house for a good, long, hot, bath. Once ready for bed, he made a mug of hot chocolate to finish off a very eventful day.

He was delighted with the way things were going at that moment. The business was running along well, and his social life was just beginning to shape up, and he was thrilled to bits with the bee keeping scenarios, and his interaction with the Oliver family, especially Mandy and her foal. His life was replete, for the moment anyway, surely nothing could go wrong and spoil it now.

The next morning was a bit chaotic as Margaret and Jenifer arranged their belongings and settled in to his home. Ray went outside very early as usual and filled in the gaps, until Margaret, was ready to bog in around the stall and garden. Mid-morning Aunt Libby came into the van and set up morning tea, and brought the day's mail with her. As usual quite a lot of it was circulars and rubbish. Then he came to one letter that looked somewhat official and more serious. He slipped the blade of his pocket knife along the top and took out a wad of official papers. He gasped as he opened it out and read the summary. His Aunt and Margaret both saw the expression on his face as he reread the front page. Almost together, Aunt Libby and Margaret, tried to speak and find out what could be so disturbing. He passed the front sheet to them in silence hoping he had misread the letter although he knew he had not.

The letter was from a firm of solicitors in Ostlay who had been asked to act on behalf of the veterinary surgeon, who was supposed to have attended Amanda's filly when she was in labour. It was a very stern letter telling Raymond that they were acting on behalf of M.C Macintosh, the veterinarian based in Ostlay. They claimed, on behalf of their client, that Ray had performed an illegal operation on a horse at the Oliver's farm. As he was not a qualified veterinary surgeon, it was a serious crime to have birthed the foal that needed a caesarean operation to extract it, in their stable or anywhere else.

He was to appear before a magistrate in the local assizes two weeks hence, where he would be charged with the offence and tried before the court. Raymond was stunned as were his Aunt and Margaret. Margaret was the first to react, and asked him what he was going to do about it. Raymond had a quick think about the problem then grinned hugely.

When the ladies asked him, "What was it he found so funny?" He told them that he had not performed any operations on the horse, or any other animal, therefore, he would attend the court as ordered and defend himself making the Vet look silly. Sure, he had manipulated the foal and filly, to safely birth the foal, and save the life of the filly, as well as the foal, but that action did not constitute an operation as such, or at least he hoped it didn't. Also, with Mr, Oliver's assistance he had saved the filly's life by raising her up, back onto her chest, then her feet. Both his Aunt Libby and Margaret, had plenty of comments about miserable, mean, and ungracious, Vets; and they couldn't believe he would even consider any such action against someone who had saved his bacon. As they said, "Imagine the publicity, and reactions of the horse fraternity, had not Raymond, fortuitously, been on site in the nick of time, and saved both the foal and her mother from almost certain death.

Raymond called his solicitors office and obtained an appointment to consult with his lawyer Mr. Wilkinson. He attended the office of Mr. Wilkinson the following morning where they shared a cup of coffee and friendly chat before Raymond told of his problem. Mr. Wilkinson agreed with him that he had no need to worry and once the facts were known, he would be exonerated provided he had evidence to back up his position. He said that he could not assist directly because this was not his field of expertise but tendered a short list of much more qualified lawyers, one of whom, should be able to assist. He told Raymond to let them know of his relationship, here, with Mr. Wilkinson as that would get him some priority. He continued with advice and told Raymond to reply immediately to the solicitor who had contacted him, and plead "NOT GUILTY". Also, he needed to gather together any supporting evidence, in writing, to qualify his remarks. He suggested that Raymond hire a good photographer to photograph the area of the horse's abdomen where the possible offence had, supposedly, taken place.

By the time he reached home, he had decided to write the letter, and he would defend himself from this ridiculous charge, without any help from the legal fraternity. He was considering contacting a photographer but opted instead to drive out and talk to the

Oliver family first, which he did. They assured him that they would all attend his trial, as would a friend of theirs, who could assure the court of his innocence. This gentleman was a qualified veterinarian surgeon and an inspector with the RSPCA, who had actually seen the filly and could confirm that no operation had taken place.

On the morning of his trial Raymond was up and about very early to organise as much of the day as he could, and get all the staff organised to fill in for himself and his Aunty, who was adamant that she would attend court with him. Margaret and Jenifer were all set to run his business whilst he was away.

After all the usual court formalities the case got underway. When asked how he wished to plead to the heinous offence, He replied, "Definitely not guilty your worship, and I am going to defend myself."

The magistrate said, "That is probably a very unwise decision young man, but you are quite at liberty to conduct your own defence."

The prosecution lawyer read out the details of the said offence, pointing out the seriousness of lay persons carrying out this sort of operation, even on their own animals, let alone someone else's animal, and charging a fee for services rendered.

When called upon to respond, Raymond called Mrs. Oliver to the witness box and quizzed her about the telephone calls that she and Amanda had made to the Veterinarian's home, to inform him of the situation, and the current need for urgent support.

When she stepped down, Raymond called Amanda Oliver to the witness box, and to save time asked her to relate as much of the morning's event as she could remember. Amanda carefully related all that had happened as the morning progressed. She told the court that at 6 o'clock or sometime very close to that she ran across the yard and into the house to get her mother to call the Vet again. Mrs Oliver, as stated, told Amanda that the Vet was out on another call. She told her that she had explained how urgent veterinary care was needed, but could do no more.

Amanda said that she had been desperate and very distraught, when she turned around addressing Raymond with the words, "I don't

241

suppose you know how to get a foal out of its mother's belly. do you? I can't even find a leg or the head. They are both going to die unless we can get the foal out quickly. I think only a caesarean section will get the foal away from her now."

Raymond admitted he had no experience with horses, but had birthed calves, and lambs, in desperate situations, so, he was prepared to have a go. As he ran across the yard, he was pulling off his outer clothes, in spite of the cold, handing them to me. I had a bucket of water and a boiling kettle in the stable ready for the Vet and a bar of antiseptic soap to sterilise his hand and arm. Once his hand and arm were clean, he inserted his hand into the birth canal and pushed it as far as he could, then he realised that my description of the foal's position was quite accurate. He could only feel the back bone but no legs he told me, and no sign of the head either."

Amanda was asked to step down and Raymond took her place on the stand. He told the magistrate how difficult the foal was to move around, but managed at last as Mr. Oliver, with some help from his daughter, managed to raise the filly onto her chest, then onto her feet, where she could breathe properly again.

Raymond then called his last witness, a Mr Robertson. The prosecution complained that they had not been warned about this witness but the magistrate overruled them. Raymond asked Mr. Robertson for his qualifications. He was indeed a qualified veterinarian surgeon, working as a field officer with the RSPCA and a friend of the Oliver's. He pointed out that he was a frequent visitor to the Oliver's farm and had, in fact called there a few days after the birth of Amanda's foal. He was proudly shown the foal and her mum and told of the drama of birthing her. Both looked well and the foal was suckling her mum. He had checked the filly and assured Amanda that she had recovered well from the ordeal of the birth. He was able to convince the court that the filly bore no signs, what-so-ever, of any operation. She bore no scars or wounds anywhere on her lower abdomen, and there were no stiches evident. Amanda assured him that the foal had been birthed in the normal way even though the presentation had seemed impossible.

At that point the Prosecution stood up again and asked the court for an adjournment, to allow him to discuss the situation with his client. The magistrate declared that, as it was close to lunch time, they would adjourn for one hour for lunch. Raymond went off with his Aunt to a nearby café for lunch before returning to court. The magistrate called the court to order and the prosecution begged forgiveness of the court, declaring that his client wished to withdraw the complaint against Raymond Clarke, and cancel the hearing. He would pay any costs incurred by the defence as well as the court. He thanked the magistrate for his time and stepped down.

The magistrate addressed Raymond with the comment, "I suppose, that your costs are minimal, young man, seeing as you adequately defended yourself from this farcical charge."

He replied, "That would appear to be the case your Honour but I did contact my solicitor Mr, Wilkinson, for advice and I have had to hire extra staff to run my business whilst I am away today. I would like to suggest that I am allowed the rest of the day at least, to check it all out. I had to drive to the Oliver's farm before-hand to check with them, and that's when I learnt about Mr. Robertson's involvement."

"Yes, all that is relevant, so I would suggest you take a few days to be sure you haven't missed anything, just drop your detailed invoice in to the clerk of courts here and he will attend to it," the magistrate said, "Thank you for your attendance here today.

Raymond and Aunt Libby drove back home and got back to work. Margaret and other staff were doing a great job holding the fort and Ray soon had everything fully stocked again. The stall was always busy about the time that the schools kicked out and mothers came to collect them and stock up as they went home to prepare dinner for their families.

Chapter Nine

Apology and Humility

Their lives settled down after the court case, and everything appeared to be running very smoothly. Ray and Melanie were enjoying outings from time to time, especially the Leeds Variety Show on Saturday evenings. Jenifer was somewhat cold towards him, but moving into farm house had lifted her spirits, and she settled down to the Mushroom business with a relish. Ray had acquired a serviceable gas fired boiler, and some pipe work, from his favourite scrap dealer, and the plumbing students at the college were assisting in its installation across the road, at Metcalf's farm. It was big enough to heat the cellars, as well as the rest of the house, and a greenhouse, if and when, one became available. The students began to build the stands and tables ready for the mushroom crop as soon as it was ready. The manager at the local markets was keen to obtain a supply of mushrooms and bottled honey, as well as any other surplus produce. He suggested to Raymond that the mushrooms were too expensive for the markets, so hopefully, would he be amenable to a wholesale discount of about 30%. Raymond claimed, and rightly so, that he could sell all that he could produce, especially out of season which it nearly always was. Raymond stated, "We never have any surplus, but once the new extensions are operating that situation might change. At the moment I have half a dozen trays that I could let you have as a trial but only at 20% discount. Andrew, finally agreed to do a deal at 20% off just this once.

The following morning Raymond called a friend who worked the markets, to see what happened. When his friend returned the call, he told Raymond that the mushrooms had in fact been eagerly snapped up, by hotels and restaurants, even though the markets had put on a substantial loading. As a result, Raymond increased the price on his stall, both retail, and possibly wholesale. The honey had also sold eagerly and much more was needed urgently. Fortunately, Raymond had a large quantity in the big barn. There were quantities of 5 varieties so he delivered a box of each to the market. The manager was delighted, but he wanted to talk some more about the mushroom supplies. Ray told him about the new boiler at Metcalf's and promised a good supply soon. He had raised his own retail prices in line with the markets and nobody complained. They were so glad to have out of season mushrooms, especially the hotels and restaurants. During these discussions Ray had a sudden impulse. He realised that as winter progressed into early spring, he would not be able to keep up supplies of some produce such as potatoes. He suggested that he get together with the market manager to discuss the possibility of helping each other. Mushrooms for spuds etc? That was soon agreed on. To share their surplus produce seemed a great idea and they agreed to give it a try.

The business settled down well after the court case. and they were very busy and everything looked rosy again. until one

Saturday morning about three weeks or so later. Ray stepped into the stall and looked out at the roadside where a dark green Range Rover was just pulling in. He recognised the vehicle immediately, and the driver, and said out loud, "Oh hell no. Not more of that, and especially on Saturday morning. I'll have to get rid of them quickly if I can."

Margaret asked, Hey, what's happened mate? What on earth has upset you like this? Your shaking all over?"

He pointed out the Range Rover and replied, "That's the vet from Ostlay that I had all that trouble with. It looks like he has brought his wife and family with him as well."

"You had better disappear, pal," Margaret stated. We'll deal with the sod and get rid of him. I'll just tell him that you are not available today. I'll tell him to phone next week and make an appointment to see you."

"No, but thanks Margaret. I'll talk to him and see why he's come. It might not be about the court case anyway. He surely wouldn't have brought his wife and two little girls with him if he was about to make trouble.

249

Knowing him he would be more likely to send his solicitor."

Because the stall was quite busy as usual, Raymond stepped outside into the driveway to meet his visitors.

He politely greeted the vet who was keen to shake hands with him, which he did. The vet apologised for interrupting him when he was obviously busy, pointing out that he had not come to make trouble. His wife had been told about the stall and was keen to see it for herself, even though it was a fair way from their home in Ostlay.

Raymond side stepped passed the vet saying, "So this lovely young lady is your wife, and these two beautiful girls are yours too."

"Yes, that's correct. This is Veronica, my wife, and these two are Ronda and Rosalind, our girls."

Raymond stepped back towards the counter and picked up a tray of sample, soft fruits and offered it to the girls, asking them if they would like to choose some to eat. The girls were a bit reticent to try some of the fruits until Veronica assured them that it was ok. She said she was keen to do her shopping and grab some of the lovely produce on display. The girls enjoyed looking around the stall, and once they got over their shyness, they chattered ten to the dozen, pouring out question after question. Ray invited the girls to go for a walk with him to see the gardens. Mum and dad were keen to look around as well, so Raymond led the way. The girls weren't keen to enter the cellars, but gasped with amazement once they saw the mushrooms popping up everywhere.

Back at the stall the ladies and students were travelling well, even though they were flat out serving and restocking with more produce. Raymond said he would leave them to it because he needed to make a quick trip across the road, where he claimed he had a special treat for the girls. He ushered them safely across and led them to the old stables. He opened the door and invited the girls to follow. Inside, there were about 1000 baby meat birds, which had just arrived earlier that morning. These were the start of his latest enterprise. Barbeque chicken was the latest fad and he wanted to be part of it. The upper stories over the stables and cow sheds in his own yard had not been needed for the laying hens and they were huge. He intended to start them off in Metcalf's stables then transfer them to his place. The little girls were delighted and carefully played with the day-old babies, whilst trying to keep their clothes clean.

After a good deal of research, he had decided on a special hybrid line of birds which he experimented with to speed up growth rates. He crossed a special white hen imported from Europe, with a line of Light Sussex cockerels and then with White leghorns until a line of cockerels from Asia were available from quarantine. The imported birds were in fact stock from fighting cocks. Their breasts were almost double the width of normal birds and developed much sooner. He wanted the finished birds to be as white as possible to make sure that any tiny feathers left after plucking would not show up on the carcass.

They had a great deal of difficulty getting the girls out of the stables and back over the road. Raymond had to apologise then and get back to work. Veronica bought a large selection of fruits and vegetables, also a number of jars of honey as well as homemade, jams, pickles, and preserves before promising to return regularly.

Early on the following Monday morning Raymond received a call from a salvage firm that he regularly had plenty of business with over time. Jeffry the owner called about a large greenhouse that needed to be removed urgently for an industrial estate on the south edge of the city, which meant that it was fairly close to the farm. He drove over there to check out the greenhouse, it was massive. He needed to negotiate quickly with the salvage people, who were getting ready to bulldoze the structure. They spent some time discussing the removal without getting much closer to the event. Raymond told them that it would be cheaper to buy a new one because of the difficulty of transport and the amount of glass breakage. The woodwork was overdue for painting and the putty needed to be replaced but he was still interested if it was cheap enough, in fact free. He had noticed that the framework was in prefabricated sections bolted together which meant it would transport easier. However, each panel would be very heavy with the glass in place. and almost impossible to handle with the possibility of many breakages and most of the glass was quite loose and likely to fall out. The site manager told him he could have it free of charge if he got it away within a week, because even if they bulldozed it there would be a mountain of broken glass to remove.

"Ok I'll take it, but we will need to remove all the glass onto pallets first," Ray declared.

"Right you are young man. You are welcome to use whatever you need on site here. There are enough pallets in that stack over there and we have a couple of forklifts to handle it. How soon can you get started on it pal?"

"How about right now? I'll drive home and collect my trailer and some troops then get started. Is one of your forklifts free for the rest of the day and can we work here all weekend? I see one of them at least is roadworthy, so I'll need to drive it to my joint to unload the pallets. Actually, I have a large tandem trailer which should be big enough to carry one of the forklifts over to my place."

"There you are then young man that was easy. My men can sort out some pallets to get you started and stack them over here nice and handy for you. You can use any of the scaffolds and stands that you need."

Raymond drove home and hitched up the trailer and collected three of his older workers and returned. Using the forklifts made it quite easy to remove the glass especially close to the ridge where it was hard to reach. Because all the putty was dried up and useless, they soon had a large section deglazed and began removing the framework. He was hoping that uncle Fred would have the weekend off to supervise and assist. He would then have to dig out and pour a concrete foundation, to sit the frames on as they were removed. A quick phone call to his friends at the trade college soon rounded up some extra help. The wood work would need rubbing down and repainting before reglazing and Uncle Fred would need help to mark out the foundations, dig away any irregularities to level the site. Raymond had an old concrete mixer, so he only needed cement, sand and gravel to mix together. A few phone calls soon organised all that and it only needed Fred to be free for the weekend, which he was.

They were able to borrow a stack of planks from the building site to form up the foundations, ready for pouring the concrete, so first thing Saturday morning the work began. Before removing any of the frames the matching joints were each numbered to make sure they were reassembled in the same place as before. The frames were cleaned, and primed, ready to paint, as they were dismantled being easier to reach. Every sheet of glass was carefully stacked on the pallets which were transported to the new site. Ray carefully loaded the oldest fork lift truck onto the trailer to take it to Metcalf's farm ready to unload the pallets from the trailer as they arrived. The amount of breakages was minimal and only a few new panes and lots of putty would be needed to rebuild. One problem did occur though. The bolts holding the frames together were very rusty and even soaking them in penetrating oil did not fully resolve the problem. They were all cup head bolts and relied on the square shank under the heads to stop them turning in the wood. The domed heads had nowhere to grip them but eventually most came loose but some had to be cut off with a hacksaw and replaced with new ones. Raymond decided to replace all the bolts with galvanised ones, with plenty of grease lashed on the threads. By end of Sunday, most of the glass and the frames were stacked at Metcalf's place awaiting reassembly. He had arranged for some of the staff to fire up the barbeques ready for knock off time and everyone was invited to join him in the barn for a feed of sausages, eggs, onions, and drinks before heading off home. His radiogram was put to good use to encourage all his friends to dance the night away. The total cost of their labours was minimal and they all agreed that a good time was had by all.

By the time that the concrete had set, and the paint dry, another week had passed, so they were ready for another marathon weekend. During the week the steam pipes and radiators had been installed by his favourite plumbers. Electricity mains were connected, and a switch board was ready to be activated. They borrowed both forklifts to make reassembly much easier, and with his uncle's expertise all went according to plan.

The demolition contractor was astounded to find the greenhouse gone, in just two days, and suggested that he could use Ray's skills and ingenuity in any future projects. Raymond told him he would need a couple more days slotted into each week to achieve that.

Some of his college pals helped to assemble the frames quickly so the forklifts could be returned ready for another week at the demolition site. Once the frames were finished, some of the scaffolding and planks used for the concrete were set up and the glass refitted. Fortunately, the end walls both had double doors and with care they were able to get one of the bobcat machines in, to change the soil regularly, and manure it.

As soon as time permitted, Ray, realised he needed to travel up to the Oliver's farm where he was sure there would be a good deal of honey ready for harvesting. He took Melanie with him to help handle the frames and speed up the operation. Whilst they were enjoying morning tea Mrs Oliver, "Anne", asked him if he could handle any more sites for his bees. He pointed out, there had been a goodly quantity of swarms during the previous summer so he had acquired many more hives, thanks to the bee boxes which the college was constantly turning out for him. He particularly needed more of the late bell heather honey, and any other that was available, so what did she have in mind. Ann told him about a good friend of the family who had a sheep run a few miles away. She also was keen to grow vegetables and fruit trees but was having little success. She said that having seen the Oliver's fruit and their flowering vegetables such as peas and beans she wondered if he could work the same magic over there.

Raymond said, "That might be ok if she has a sheltered site that we can use. As we have finished here for today, we could run over there now and check out the site. The late honey we can always do with, but like I said with you, it all depends on having a sheltered corner to site the hives early in the year. You had better give me some, directions."

Amanda told him, "Drive up over the next ridge and down into the valley for about 5 miles. I need to take Monarch for a run today.

I'll meet you at the road end and lead you in. It's quite easy to find the lane on your right-hand side. It won't take more than a few minutes to saddle up and get going and it's not far for me over the moor. Turning to Melanie she asked, "Do you ride at all?"

"Oh yes, I do, but I have to hire a horse because I don't own one, and we have nowhere to keep one either." Melanie told her.

"Ok then you ride Bella, I'll ride Monarch. Bella will be good for you since she's already had a good run, and I have a spare helmet in the tack room. You are already wearing jeans and boots, so you should be right. Hop up now and get a feel for her while I saddle up. We may need to adjust the stirrups because you are so tall." Melanie mounted and moved around the yard, getting the feel of Bella's gait while she was waiting, then they were off. Ray went for a quick check around the orchard and gardens with Anne before heading off down the track. The girls were waiting at the road junction when he got there and cantered off along the road, which soon became little more than a track. They led him into a secluded dell, which was the Morrison's homestead. Amanda introduced everyone and Ray took the girls for a stroll around the area. The dell was similar to Oliver's and was backed by a limestone cliff, much higher than the Oliver's one, but not quite so long. It was not fully facing into the sun unfortunately, but it would do the job quite nicely. and there were some solid stone buildings scattered around as well as the substantial, two storied house and barn. He asked Gwen and Robert if they could build a barrier wind break at both ends using steel posts and bales of straw. He had access to free straw bales and offered to bring them up with the hives if Bob had some steel posts and old wire netting to wrap them in. Then it was back to the house for the inevitable tea and cake, before heading off home. The girls cantered off across the moor to meet up at Oliver's road end. Melanie was thrilled with her morning on the moor, but now it was back to work. Raymond reminded her that life wouldn't always be so free and easy, and she would have to meander up there in her little car on her days off, if she wanted to enjoy Bella. She told him that it

261

would work out a lot cheaper than fees at the riding school.

The next visit to Oliver's farm, he hooked the trailer on behind with a load of straw bales and six hives full of bees. They went right up the moor to Morrison's place first so the bees could be let out as soon as possible. Once the hives were in place Robert attacked the wind break. The ground was extra hard with plenty of rock but they did manage a solid wall to break most of the wind. That was it for now, time for the bees to work their magic and settle in before next spring. Raymond assured the Morrisons that he would soon be back to collect the first harvest and set the hives up for the autumn crop of bell heather honey. Then it was back to the Oliver's place to harvest the crop of honey, and once again he was delighted with the yield from only six hives and decided to leave two new hives up there as well, to catch any new swarms.

Back at the farm it was all go. The new greenhouse needed to be planted up and fertilised and the heater run and checked. The meat birds were growing at an alarming rate so he had to organise a couple of plucking machines and work out a marketing strategy. He believed, and rightly so, that his existing commercial customers would be able to absorb most of the early production, after which he would need to approach the take-away trade to move the rest. He and the college students were building a boiler system to cook up the offal etc. and any of the old layer birds to be turned into feed for his growing herd of pigs. This would reduce the cost of feed for the pigs and clean up the rubbish as well.

The vet and his family from Ostlay were becoming regular customers at the stall and Veronica suggested that he should set up a stall in Ostlay, a couple of days each week. Raymond pointed out some of the problems of getting itinerant trader's permission. Veronica said there was no real competition in Ostlay, and one of the village shops was their only source of produce, which proved to be expensive and somewhat less than quality produce. Raymond had a good look around the village for a suitable site off the road, and realised that the yard and parking area at the

Veterinary surgery was the most suitable, and there was sufficient room to operate a mobile shop from the ford trader van, which could be spared two days each week. He ran that idea past Andrew and Veronica, who were quite happy with the deal so long as the council would allow it, which they did. Monday and Thursday were agreed on as these days were possibly the most suitable for Raymond. He agreed to be there about 10am each day and possibly leave about 3pm. Hopefully that would give him enough time to satisfy the citizens. There would be a lot of trial and error initially. The trader van had removable panels in the side walls set in rubber grommets which could be pushed outwards and new standard glass panels bought from the ford dealer could be installed in their place

From the first day, all went very well because Veronica had put up notices in the surgery, and other suitable venues, such as the post office, and public houses, and the café. Everyone was keen to help, especially the cafes, and hotels, to relieve them of the trouble of supply. Ray soon realised that he had underestimated how much stock he would need; and even the eggs, honey and preserves disappeared quickly. He had sold out by 2pm and promised to do better the next time. The village store keeper had come along to check out the competition and he approached Ray for a wholesale supply, which he could sell in his shop during the days that the van was not there. Ray was delighted with that arrangement and took an order for all the bottled products, as well as fresh fruit and vegetables. Veronica wrote out an addendum to the notices hoping to alert the people that he would bring much improved stocks in future. Sure enough, the next visit to the surgery, he loaded the van to maximum and once again he virtually sold out of most products quite quickly. He was approached to operate the van on Sundays due to the visitors coming into the region. He realised there might be some opposition from the churches in the town, so he limited the stall to coincide with the end of morning services to keep the peace. A self-pick market garden was operating near Harewood at the weekends which created a precedence, and should make things easier for Ray. One of his employees was a competent driver and good with the customers. Ray asked him if he would like to drive the van to Ostlay and run the stall. Gregory was as keen as mustard and took over for the next run. He suggested hooking the trailer on the back to carry more bulk supplies, such as bags of potatoes and carrots. Gregory was also interested in working with the bee hives to relieve his boss of that time-consuming task. Ray designed and built a set of steps with hand rails to enter the rear of the van and asked Gregory to leave them somewhere safe at the vet's place. Gregory soon settled down to operate the stall at Ostlay and combined that with his bee keeping duties. He really enjoyed working with the bee hives and kept the honey flowing freely.

A few months after the new hot house saga, Ray, received a big shock and a pleasant surprise. One morning, as he and flash walked over the road to check the boiler and crops before feeding the laying hens and collecting eggs. He bumped into Mrs. Metcalf who came rushing out of the house to join him. She was in a rare old state and grabbing his arm pulled him into the farm house saying, "It's Frank, I can't wake him. I think he might have died in the night. Will you come up and check him for me please? After rushing upstairs Raymond could find no vital signs of life and Franks hand was quite cold. It appeared that Frank had indeed passed away quietly during the night. Raymond went back down stairs and called the doctor, who came quickly but he could only write out a death certificate for Frank and organise the local undertaker to attend. Ray helped Anette to arrange and run the funeral and the wake. He was getting quite good at this, but each time he lost another of his dear friends in the process.

After Frank's funeral, Anette, asked him to drive her into town to meet her accountant and solicitor at the solicitor's office. He expected to drop her off and wait until she was ready to return home. However, Anette insisted that he accompany her to the meeting because it concerned him as well. After all the formalities were completed the solicitor turned to Raymond saying, "I suppose you are concerned about your part in all this young man, you have become so involved with the Metcalf farm and have invested a great deal of time and money there, but you have no cause to worry. Everything is in hand, provided you wish to carry on as you are doing now. Apparently, you did a great job organising the funeral and wake. You would have no doubt realised by now, there are no obvious relatives on either side of Mrs Metcalf's family, but fortunately Frank, and Annette here, visited me about 1953 to write out a will, two in fact, one each and they carefully allowed the script to cover either or, or both, becoming deceased, first. In appreciation of your involvement in their affairs, the wills favour yourself as the only beneficiary. I suggested at that time that, if they were truly certain that you would look after them, and their business, they anonymously vest all their property in your name, to save you any taxation problems later on. However, I persuaded them to include certain provisos regarding the remaining member of the partnership. I believe you had a similar arrangement with Mrs Osbourne which went exceptionally well. The statutory time period for death duties and gift taxes has lapsed, so you receive all these assets free of gift duty and death duties. I now require you to carefully read the addenda to the Metcalf's wills and sign here. You will be bound over to attend the remaining party, provide adequate accommodation, and sustenance, under my supervision. I have been watching your stewardship throughout your association and I am satisfied that you will continue to do so for as long as necessary. The value of their assets has increased markedly in recent years, in part due to your stewardship, whereas other properties around here have not done so well. I have no hesitation in telling you, that you are now the outright owner of the Metcalf's property, subject to probate inquiry, with the provisos set out herewith."

"Congratulations young man. I realise you have been running the property for quite a long time, and taking full responsibility for repairs and maintenance of said property, and have been a great help to Mr. and Mrs. Metcalf along the way. You richly deserve this windfall, and due to total lack of any possible claimants, this is a great outcome."

Raymond drove Mrs. Metcalf home, and over refreshments, she asked him how he felt at that moment. After considerable thought he replied, "Absolutely stunned Mrs, M., I never expected any of this but I am deeply relieved that it has worked out this way. I dearly want to look after you and this property until your dying day. It is a great honour and privilege to be given this task at so early an age, and I promise that you will never regret your decision to bestow this on me. In addition, it will allow me time to recoup most of my investments here. My only regret is that we had to lose another of my dear friends before it could happen. I'm already missing our old friend Frank. I have so enjoyed our walks around the farm together.

So back to work across the road, and as usual the crew had excelled their selves. They always seemed to do better when he was away, even for a short while, just to show him how much they respected him. However, his relationship with Melanie was cooling off for some reason and it bothered him. They had got along together for a long time and he was considering proposing marriage to her.

Chapter Ten

Surprise and Disappointment

One morning Ray went into the main cellar under the big house to check out the mushroom crops, when he came upon Melanie who was working down there. She seemed to be weeping quietly as she worked, and did not even hear his approach until he spoke, asking her, "What is the matter my love?" She burst into sobs in his arms and real tears began to pour down her cheeks at his words, and she quickly became inconsolable. He let her go on until she began to rally herself. As she stood back away from him, she rubbed her belly before blubbering; "Oh Raymond, you are going to hate me. I'm expecting a baby as you can see."

"How can that be Melanie?" he asked. "We have never done anything to bring that on have we. Oh God Mel, this could not possibly be my baby, so, who is the father? I have never done any of that with any girl, let alone you. I am still a virgin, and I swear I have never done anything other than kiss you."

"Apart from you Raymond, I have never been out with any boys, other than Gregory so it must be his. No, don't ask me, I am sure he did not use any method to protect me. We only did it a couple of times you see."

"Oh! Mel you are a silly girl, only once is enough to impregnate you on the right day. Thank goodness I have found out your infidelity this early; shame on you. Have you told Gregory yet, and what about your parents? They will be so disappointed in you. You must go and tell Gregory at the earliest chance, today if possible and Mom and Dad tonight."

"Yes, you are right: Dad will kill me."

"I very much doubt that Mel because it will serve no purpose what-so-ever. He, like me, will be bitterly disappointed in you, and he will almost certainly rant, and rave, and shout at you. If he uses violence against anyone it will likely be against Gregory. I suggest you go and see Greg now and when you two get yourselves sorted come and talk things over with me. I have a few ideas to alleviate some of the problems that will occur. Work wise you have both performed well for me and are valuable assets to my business. You have all the skills and experiences to assist me every day and I will find it difficult to replace either of you in the short term, let alone both of you."

"What will I do if Gregory doesn't want to marry me, Raymond?"

"Not my problem, Mel, I'll sort out any staff problems that occur, but no more than that."

"Oh my God: what a mess? I thought you would sack us both straight away. Thank you for being so understanding Raymond."

"Gregory is working over at Metcalf's so get away over there now and get this sorted, then get back here quick because we are desperately short of stock. I'll take these that you have ready for now, but I need buttons and large field immediately. The rest of this mess we can sort out later"

"Yes, Raymond, I am so sorry. I will make this up to you somehow, thank you." With that she left the cellar and headed over the road. Some little time later he spotted her returning back to the cellar door, and returning to work. He left it for an hour or so whilst he caught up with his thoughts, and there was a slight gap in customers when he handed the stall over to Margaret, before returning to the cellar to collect more stock and check on Mel. A very subdued young lady greeted him, handing over a sizeable quantity of button mushrooms, freshly picked, then looking into his eyes she said, "I did as you asked me Ray, and after he got over the shock, Gregory asked me to marry him. We are going to my home together to see Mum and Dad after work. Greg is nearly finished at Metcalf's and will talk to you then."

"Ok Mel, I'll stay with you now and try to catch up in here, then you need to start in the cottage cellar to stock up for the hotel rush in the morning. After that we'll work out a plan to deal with this problem of yours. When Mel moved over to the cottage cellar, Ray wandered over the road for a chat with Mrs. Metcalf. Annette had the kettle on the boil as usual, and as soon as they were settled at the table with a cup of tea each, and a plate full of cakes and biscuits she asked. "To what do I owe the pleasure of this visit in the middle of a busy day."

"He replied, "Well Annette, I need a favour from you. You know Melanie, of course, and I have just found out that she is expecting a baby. Gregory has agreed to marry her so I want to discuss accommodation with you."

"Why is Gregory going to marry Mel? I realised a few weeks ago that she was with child, although I didn't think you or she was aware of her condition. I expected to attend your wedding with her not Gregory. I thought she was your girl, Ray."

"Point taken Annette, I thought so too. But she and I have never laid together. I have never had "those, sort of relationships," with her, or anyone else for that matter. I value both of their input to my business and wish that to continue. I wanted to ask you if you would consider changing your house around, like the two over the road, to create a suitable dwelling for them. This house is so large and really needs people living in it."

"Yes Ray, you are quite right, but it is your house now to do with as you please. It will be good to have company around me as time goes by. Oh, my goodness I am just realising I will have a baby in the house at last. Frank and I tried desperately to have a little one but it was not to be. I became pregnant a number of times but miscarried each time. It was so upsetting for both of us that we decided not to try again. This is the best news I've had for a long time, and I only wish my Frank was still around to share it with me. Oh Yes Ray, please do what needs to be done and I'll work around it until it's finished." With that she jumped up moved around the table and gave Ray a huge cuddle and a few kisses, leaving him somewhat stunned in disbelief.

He went back home and continued with his day's work. Late afternoon on school days were always busy as Mums collected their kids from school. At the end of the day they needed to have sufficient stock to start the next morning. This was particularly necessary when frosty nights and early mornings were the order of the day. Gregory and Mel tentatively sought him out when they finished for the day. They found him in the hen house collecting the last of the day's eggs. He asked them, "Well have you pair of clowns sorted out your immediate problems".

"Yes, sorry about all this mess boss. We have decided that we wanted to get married any way, regardless of the baby, but that only makes the next bit more difficult. We will have to find somewhere to live for starters. Neither of us want to live with parents and in-laws and housing around this area is impossible, neither private, nor public."

"Well I have good news on that front, because as well as a house of some sort you will need to furnish it, and set it up with everything that you need to make it a home. I have a possible answer to most of that but it will mean a lot of work. You have both been inside my home to some extent and I suggest you two do the same. Mrs. Metcalf is living in that massive house over the road, and with a little bit of capital, which I will supply, we can convert it into a delightful apartment house for the three of you. Uncle Freddy can change the rooms

277

around to make a kitchen, extra bathroom and toilets as he did with my two houses. There's ample furniture available, some in there and more in the two attics at my place. A jolly good clean out, some spit and polish, and a lick of paint, most of which you can do yourselves and you are all set. How would that work out for you both. No travelling, no bus fares, no water bills, gas bills or electricity bills. I would suggest we settle on a fixed weekly rental to cover all your expenses. The capital works would come out of my taxation account called, Staff housing. Now off you go and sort out this mess with your parents, and tell me the outcome in the morning, and don't be late."

Gregory replied, "We don't deserve any of that boss, but we'll gladly accept it and work like slaves from now on to justify your trust in us. Thank you Raymond this will make the next interview a lot easier on everyone." Then shaking Ray's hand, he headed home.

Recovering from her shock Mel threw herself at him, and hugged the life out of him, saying, "Thanks Ray, I love you. I promise that we will never forget this day, and you will never regret your generosity. You can be the baby's God Father."

Off they went to face the music at home, first Melanie's parents then Gregory's. Ray finished off a few jobs and wandered off home to a lonely house and a heap of paperwork. Jenifer was just walking into his kitchen with a tray of dinner for him. She pulled the kettle over the hob on the Aga for a hot drink. "Mom thought you might be ready for this. She reckons you've had a bad day. Did you?"

"Yes, I certainly did Jenifer. Oh; heck you might as well know the truth now because you'll soon hear versions of it anyway. Melanie and Gregory have been going together, and Mel is expecting. They have decided to get married and will live over the road, once we renovate it like this house."

"Well when you have a bad day you really go at it don't you? You must be shattered. I take it you are going to keep them both on here. You really need them, especially Gregory."

"That's true enough mate, and now I'll need a new soul mate, but not immediately. The arrangements I have with you and Margaret are so precious. I'm surrounded by beautiful girls every day, but I shall be wary of them in the future."

"You look like you could do with a nice cosy cuddle, Ray, is it alright if I give you one?"

"Yes love, I should maybe have gone with you instead of Mel in the first place. Oh, what a mess they've created. I just hope it all goes well with their parents. Come on then sweetheart let's have that cuddle, then I'll eat this lovely meal Margaret has prepared for me before it spoils. I am still too numb to appreciate anything at the moment, even food, but I'm starving. So saying, he ate the dinner and washed the dishes. Jenifer went off to her bed, and he to a good, long, hot, soak in the tub.

He awoke early the next morning after a restless night. Day was just dawning as he looked out of his window. To his surprise Mel's little car was just pulling into the yard. He watched as both Mel and Greg alighted hugged and kissed, separated, one to the cellar, the other across the road. Soon the noise of a small engine told him Greg was digging carrots. After a couple of mugs of his favourite beverage, tea of course, and a few slices of Margaret's homemade bread heavily laden with crystalized honey, he went to tackle his world. At least it was HIS world and no-one could take it from him, or so he thought. If there were any faults in it, he only had himself to blame; it was all his own doing. At a reasonable hour, he took his sketch pad over to see Annette and measure up her little world. He gave her a kiss and cuddle and consumed another cup of tea while they chatted then got started. Hopefully his uncle would be available once again, and some of the new crop of students from the college. They enjoyed working on real projects rather than imaginary ones. They could look back on the finished project with pride and satisfaction.

Greg and Mel worked hard all week, esp- ecially on Friday, to get ahead with harvesting the various crops, to leave the weekend free to attack the house. To Ray's amazement, Mel's parents came with her, carrying cleaning gear and a vacuum cleaner. Shortly after, Greg's parents arrived on their own, because Greg was already working in the garden, whilst awaiting their arrival. Just at that moment Uncle Fred walked over the road ready to get started. He and Ray had spent some time during the week surveying and measuring the rooms. The house needed very little modification. They would have to build some stud walls to create the bathroom and toilet and the only destruction of the existing infrastructure was a couple of extra doorways. Only three students turned up to give a hand but that was more than enough at that stage. The laundry wasn't a problem because it was huge, with plenty of room for two washers and driers. It had originally been used as a dairy where the cream was separated and churned into butter. Uncle Fred only needed to carve a hole in one wall and fit a ventilator. It is quite astonishing how much a dozen people can achieve in one day and with another day on Sunday most of the major works would be complete leaving mainly, more painting and decorating. The ladies had worked miracles on the curtains and other linens which they would re-hang once the painting was complete. At Raymond's side of the road, they discovered a kitchen table and chairs and a comfortable lounge suite needing only cleaning. There were heaps of pots, pans, cutlery and all the other bits and pieces necessary to compliment a good kitchen, once Uncle Frank had one available, along with an assortment of bowls, vases, and dishes.

Annette was in and out all the time constantly brewing tea, cooking scones and cakes, baking bread and making it into sandwiches. She was really enjoying her day of activity.

Ray was keeping a low profile, and as soon as the stall slowed down around lunch time, he jumped in the transit van and headed for Mabel's place. Once he could see that Margaret and Jenifer were coping well with the morning trade he wasn't needed. He had been so busy of late that he had neglected to call and spend time with Mabel and he was surprised how much she had achieved. Ray had settled two of the younger girls up there with her to learn the honey trade, working with Mabel, bottling and preserving fruit and vegetables for sale, and assisting Mabel so she didn't get too bogged down with all the extra work. Mabel felt a need to remove the travelling time for the girls so, offered to allow them to board with her during the week. There were two spare bedrooms and a small lounge going begging, so they were happy to settle in with her. Ray had been sending all the bent and twisted or slightly damaged fruit and vegetables up to Mabel each day expecting most of them to go as feed for her animals but she, with the help of the girls, was turning much of it into pickles, chutney and relish. She had ordered special labels and jars, and already had a van load to take back with the honey. She presented him with an account for payment for jars labels and other consumables, which he accepted from her. There was enough in the van to cover all the bills and more, and he needed the stock for the stall. He asked her to continue with the pickles, preserves and honey as long as she had ingredients to fill them. As he was about to climb into his van, she called out to him, "Just a moment Ray, one more thing. A dear old acquaintance of me and my husband has continued to call here, mainly for honey, and we had a long chat the other day. He knows about you and your business and he would like to see you when you have time. He is a retired surgeon from the hospital, and lives on a small holding out near Skelton, and they have lots of fruit. They wondered if you might be interested, although it's a fair way to travel. You would also need to pick the fruit yourself because he cannot manage the ladders any more, due to an accident. I have written his details on this bit of paper in case you are interested."

"Ok thanks for that Mabel I'll ring him and maybe go for a run out there for a look-see. Thanks for the info. I'll let you know what happens." He drove off home deep in thought. I do need more fruit but do I need any more work? I might have to take on more help. Greg's younger brother had been asking him if there were any jobs going and that might be the way to go. He often turned up to see Greg and always pitched in with any work that was happening. He had always worked at a steady job since leaving school, and would probably camp with Greg to save travelling so much. Ray called in to see Greg and Melisa and their baby boy. Alister had just arrived before him so they were able to discuss the job. Alister

285

had a driver's licence and was familiar with tractors. Like his brother he seldom drank any alcoholic drinks and had a clean licence. Greg and Melisa were quite agreeable for him to live with them initially to save travelling. Ray was happy to engage Alister as soon as he was free from his current job. It was Alister who raised another issue. He said that he and Greg had an older sister, Elizabeth who was in some trouble. She needed a decent job and somewhere to live because her husband had disappeared without trace and left her with two little children. Ray pushed that information aside for now to concentrate on Alister, who he had decided would fit in well.

Just after lunch the next day Ray noticed a strange car pulling into the driveway. I say strange because he now knew all the locals and their vehicles. Weekends, especially Sunday there were often strangers around but seldom mid-week. This was a late model dark blue Jaguar. The driver struggled out of the door and hobbled around to the passenger door and opened it before helping his white-haired passenger to alight. They were both having some difficulty walking up to the stall. Ray greeted them with his usual cheery greeting and big smile, before saying, "Good afternoon and welcome to my stand. Did you have something in mind or just looking around. I have other products in the refrigerator and freezer inside. I have fresh dressed whole meat birds as well as frozen ones and some delicate fruits in the fridge."

The gentleman introduced themselves as Mr. and Mrs. Braithwaite from Skelton. He admitted that he had been talking to Mabel Featherstone and was hoping Ray might be able to help them. Ray said, "Ok Mr. Braithwaite Tell me about your problems. I may be able to help."

"Please call me Lionel. We have a very large orchard with mainly apples. A large area of berry fruits and a few acres of grassland. I had a bad fall early in the year and as you can see, I have difficulty even walking let alone climbing ladders. I would like you to come out to our place and see what you can salvage. Money isn't our problem; I just hate to see all that fruit going to waste, and it looks like you can use

287

some of it if we manage to harvest it in time. Will you come? The apples are mainly Bramley and that is another problem that you must have as well, thanks to the E.E.C.? Will you have time to spare, please?

"Yes, ok, early tomorrow morning. I'll reorganise my crews and set off as early as we can. We should be there shortly after daybreak so put the kettle on."

"Ok that's better than we expected and the kettle is always on." Replied his wife, Ethel.

It doesn't take much to mess up a day's schedule, thought Ray, as he set off to organise his staff and himself. He sent a staff member to the nearest service station where he ran a credit account, to fill up the Zephyr car. He asked Margaret and Jenifer to make up a large quantity of sandwiches and pack them up ready. Margaret and Aunty Libby were to manage the stall with a couple of juniors to help. He, Jenifer, Kathy, and two of the junior members of staff. would set off very early and drive, first to Mabel's and pick up her and her girls, Katy and Mary, then cut across to Skelton and hope to find the Braithwaite's place. Mabel decided to take her own van along as well and filled it with a quantity of trays and boxes, then they were off, Ray led the way in the big van which he loaded with an assortment of boxes and trays.

The small holding was not hard to find, but Ray got the surprise of his life when he arrived. He soon had his crew hard at work, picking Berries onto trays that stacked together in Mable's van. Ray himself went to look for their hosts and immediately commented on the fact that the house appeared to have two front entranceways. Lionel admitted that the house was actually two separate cottages although they had an internal connecting door, as well as the external front doors. He told Ray they had never had any use for the other half and it had sat empty for many years. They had tried to rent it out but it was a bit remote for most people, but Ray got his brain working and reckoned that he might have a solution.

Ray had a good look around and found a large bed of rhubarb ready for picking; as were a few late plums, and a tree or two of early apples. By the time that the light was fading the big van and Mabel's small van were fully loaded. Mabel was to unload all the selected fruit in her van, at her place for jam making and preserves. The big van they took home and unloaded, some straight into the stall, the rest to store in the barn. He admitted to his staff that they had enjoyed a very pleasant and profitable day. After a couple of weeks, Ray intended to take the picking platforms, he now had two, on the tandem trailer, and return to start picking the Bramley apples. Lionel had told him that the markets would no longer handle the Bramleys because of the E.E.C. ruling so he was stuck with them, but Ray was still happy to sell them direct to his retail customers and to heck with the E.E.C. During the next two weeks, Ray spend as much time as possible trying to sort out his staff. Alister was due to start with him the week that he arranged to begin picking apples at Skelton, and had moved in with his brother Greg. That left the problem of Elizabeth. She needed somewhere decent to live and school for the kids, as well as a day job between school times. He rang Ethel with a query: did a school bus pass by the cottages. The answer came back affirmative, yes it did. Greg and Melisa had two cars between them, and Alister had an ancient Norton motor cycle with a side car attached. Elizabeth had a driver's licence. Ray hoped he had a solution to Elizabeth's immediate problems, so he took half a day off and drove out to see the Braithwaites.

He discussed the problems of housing his staff, and Ethel took him on a tour of the cottage next door. Sure, it was smothered in thick dust but otherwise it was sound. There were no signs of water incursions, so all it needed was a thorough spring clean, New curtains and rugs some lino and carpets. and a few bits of furniture to make it into a home. There was still lots of furniture and other needs in the three attics at his place, even some quite usable curtains, and some linen, that a session in the washing machine would put back into use. He discussed the long-term future of the Braithwaites lives, and although they loved living where they were now, it had become obvious that they would need to move closer to amenities and medical services in the near future; or rather, immediately. They had offered the small holding for sale but no-one seemed interested, not even the realtor. Ray still had plenty of funds and assets left due to his inheritances and compensation so he put a couple of propositions forward. He discussed Elizabeth renting the empty cottage. Then he talked about leasing the property himself, with or without an option to purchase it outright. Lionel told Ray that they had an offer of a unit close to all amenities on the edge of a small town, but they had to settle the farm first. They couldn't afford to just abandon the farm and they couldn't move on unless they managed to sell it. A lease deal would help but was not ideal.

"Ok, then you two, stated Ray, you had a valuation of some sort when you were trying to sell the property, what did that amount to?"

They dug out the real estate papers, which fortunately were no longer legally valid, and began working from there. Ray thought the valuation was a bit high for such a remote property and although the main house was up to scratch, the cottage would need a sizable cash injection and a lot of Uncle Fred's ingenuity and hard graft to bring it up to modern requirements. After a long discussion and many cups of tea they agreed on a fair and equitable valuation. Ray eventually set off home with his mind working ten-to-the-dozen.

The following day he went to see his solicitor, Mr. Wilkinson to sort out the nitty gritty. He agreed to chauffer him out to view the property and discuss the suggested price. He agreed with Ray, that Ray had got the better of the deal, and agreed to draw up the papers. Also, he reminded Ray that he needed quite a lot of tax deductions to reduce his income tax; therefore, better to spend it on staff housing and building repairs, like this, rather than dump it in the government's coffers He also agreed to act on behalf of the Braithwaites in their new venture. A copy of the title deeds was mandatory and available curtesy of the real estate firm, so he left it all in his hands. When he arrived home, he organised Greg and Alister to collect Elizabeth and deliver her to his house that evening.

Once they were all settled, he put a number of propositions before them. He suggested that Elizabeth and Alister move out to the property at Skelton and live there, either together, or separately, once the cottage was refurbished, inside and out. He wanted them to work together and run the orchard and gardens with lots of input from Ray and staff. He said there would always be enough work for Elizabeth to keep her busy between school times with seasonable help from the whole crew at busy times, and Alister could work with the main crew at each, and all the properties as needed. Elizabeth was very keen, and reckoned it would be great for her kids as well, so Ray agreed to drive them all out there on the Sunday morning with a view to setting out a plan of action. The kids went crazy. They had never been to the countryside let alone lived there. Even riding to school on a bus was going to be an exciting novelty. By the time they returned to town, Elizabeth was ready to give it a go. Time was set aside for the next weekend, to get started making the cottage habitable. Uncle Fred and two of his mates had a couple of wet days during the week and had already attacked the structural work.

At the weekend Greg, Alister and Elizabeth headed off out with cleaning gear, paint brushes etc. Their parents also joined in the fun and by Monday morning the cottage was almost ready to move into. The hot water system in the fire back worked well after a good clean out and the old bottled gas stove was usable again. A few tiles in the bath room and kitchen thanks to Uncle Fred and co. and they left the paint to dry until the next weekend. A busy bee was organised in the evenings to sort out the three attics to find furniture and utensils, which they loaded into the transit van for Ray to deliver.

One problem confronting the Braithwaites was their flock of poultry, which they could not take with them to town. Once they saw the children and their absolute delight with the hens and ducks, they offered to leave them behind for the family. Elizabeth was more than happy to accept them and promised to care for them. The pigs were taken to market and sold.

It was only in the first days of occupancy that the kids went running into the house shouting their heads off, yelling and screaming, as they searched for their mother. Elizabeth hurried outside to see what all the fuss was about. She was surprised to see a fluffed-up, speckled mother hen clucking and cackling madly. She was clucking and hissing and rushing towards the kids with wings spread wide and kicking up a heck of a fuss. Elizabeth noticed something hiding under the old hen and realised that she had a large clutch of baby chickens under her wings. It was hard to count them, but she could see there was about a dozen of the little blighters, coming out of a nest in the hedge bottom. Her kids were delighted and vowed to look after them. The pig sties were now empty, so they rounded them up into one of them and locked them up, safe from foxes and hawks until they got a bit bigger. In there they would be easier to look after, warm, and safe. Only the mother hen could escape over the door or wall leaving the chicks snug and warm inside awaiting her return, and where the kids could feed, love and water them.

The children were picked up at the front gate and taken to school and back on school days. Elizabeth tackled the housework, gardening, and the orchard during the daytime. Ray arrived after a few days to clean up the grass and weeds then plough up the two 10-acre fields ready for more fruit trees and lots of vegetables. He went over to the agricultural college and obtained a good quantity of berry bushes and more fruit trees. There was a fair amount of pig manure rotting away by the sheds and he moved a few loads of hen manure from the home property and rotary hoed it all into the ground and existing orchards. He moved many trailer-loads of cow manure from Fairweather's dairy farm. Each time he went over to the new place he took a load of manure and piled it in a heap to rot. Every time he went, the kids dragged him out to the barn to see the baby chickens. One day they were all excited because one of the ducks who had been missing ever since their arrival suddenly appeared from further away in the hedge bottom followed by 15 babies. The ducks were rounded up safely in the other pig sty where they could be fed and looked after properly. Some weeks after moving to town Lionel met up with Ray at the stall. Ray told him about the chickens and ducks and he was surprised because they hadn't ever had anything like that happen. He was amazed that the hens had gone clucky this late in the year. Then he remembered a friend of theirs who had also moved into a townsite nearby, quite some time before their move. The elderly couple took their hens with them to town, but it soon became clear that the hens were welcome, but the two roosters were not. She had begged Ethel to give the roosters a home, and also the drake, which she willingly agreed to. It was late in the summer but the roosters had not been informed of that problem, and immediately got around to doing what roosters do best, hence the broods of youngsters late in the season, much to the delight of the kids. Ray suggested that Lionel should take Ethel out to the farm one day and see for themselves. Not only the chicks but the cottages and gardens as well. Elizabeth welcomed the elderly couple, as did the kids, and it became a regular outing for them.

Chapter Eleven

Love and Marriage

During the time since Melisa's desertion of him, Ray, was taking his time to study up the situation regarding the opposite sex. After Mel's defection he was very wary of any romantic nuances around his life but he was so lonely, especially in the evenings, once the day's work was done. He was spending much more time in Jenifer's company since they lived in the same house, and she was looking after some of his daily needs along with her mother. They often spent evenings watching the television together and playing chess. On a number of occasions, Ray took her out to the Leeds City Varieties after a classy meal at one of his favourite restaurants. Eventually he realised that they spent so much time together, that maybe they ought to get engaged and possibly married. As a result, he finally got around to asking Jenifer if she would like to marry him. Jenifer was delighted and couldn't wait for it to happen. She said she had waited long enough already, so they went into town one afternoon and he bought her a smashing diamond engagement ring. Whilst in the jeweller's shop they picked out a gold wedding ring and had it engraved with the words, "Love Always".

Naturally Margaret was thrilled and began organising her daughter's wedding day.

There was very little to organise because they already had most of their needs. Ray arranged for his favourite restaurant to cater for the event, and the local Vicar was amenable to arrange the service. The day was set for only one month hence and all their friends were rounded up for the big day. Neither of them had much in the way of relatives, but all their staff were invited and many of their business clients and suppliers as well. Neither of them had been away from the farm since their first meeting but how could they get away now. As it turned out a short honeymoon quickly became a possibility. Greg and Mel both offered to hold the fort as did Margaret and Aunty Libby. Alister travelled in with Elizabeth and the kids in the side-car, much to their delight, and with Mabel and her girls in the background, they were all set. Anette was delighted to mind all the kids and cook up a storm. There seemed to be little to be gained by travelling afar, for a short honeymoon of only two weeks so Ray had booked a suite at the Grand Hotel in Scarborough, overlooking the ocean. As a school kid he had been to Scarborough a number of times on day trips with his Sunday school class, but never stayed there.

The Grand hotel was just that, and they were allocated a suite on the upper floor giving them magnificent views of the harbour, right along the southern shore line and the ruins of the castle to the north. On wet, cold days they hopped on the frunicular tram to descend to the promenade at the southern end of which was Gala land. Gala land was a huge majestic limestone cave system which housed a large funfair and even a rollercoaster, Close to the entrance a huge cavern, set on one side there was a huge grotto set up as a concert hall, with a large fully equipped stage area and dressing rooms. They held free concerts there every day, even full symphony concerts, with full orchestras. The limestone roof echoed and magnified the sounds and produced a fantastic medium. Families could stay in there all day long to avoid the inclement weather.

Fine, sunny days were gorgeous and they took advantage of the open, horse drawn, carriages that plied for trade along the sea front and around the town. Their favourite ride was around the castle headland and on to the North Shore where there was a miniature railway, boating lake and many other attractions. Alongside the harbour there was a row of food stalls selling a dazzling array of sea food delicacies such as crabs, lobster, whelks, shrimps and cockles. Most of the fore shore was lit up at night with coloured lights and entertaining tableaus. From the upper floors of the Grand it was a magnificent display, as it was also at ground level. They walked arm in arm along the sea front after dinner on fine evenings, secure in their love for each other and munching an assortment of sea food delicacies.

All good things must come to an end, so on the second Saturday they enjoyed a glorious drive in one of the horse-drawn carriages before driving home across the Yorkshire Wolds and through the historic city of York. Ray in the Zephyr, drove along in bright sunshine all the way home, with Jenifer snuggled up alongside him. They stopped in front of the stall and were immediately swamped by the kids who were playing shops and helping their mums to serve the customers and clean up any spilt cabbage leaves. Mel assured them that they had coped quite well without the love birds, so Ray and Jenifer left them to it whilst they unpacked their belongings and sorted out the presents for the kids. Ray loaded up the big van before taking a trip out to catch up with Mabel. As he was about to leave Jenifer came rushing out to join him, declaring, "I might as well come with you, there's nothing to do here. The house is all spick and span ready for us, so, let's get cracking. Where are we going, anyway?"

"Mabel's place first, then on to Skelton." He replied. At Mabel's place they hugged and greeted each other before the usual tea ceremony. Mabel apologised for still being at home instead of minding the stall but Ray told her there was no need, everything was going well at the moment. At Skelton Gardens, as Ray now called it, they were surprised to see many more chickens trotting along behind the old hens. It seemed the roosters really had been busy, too busy for winter anyway, so they put out some feed and managed to catch the both of them and lock them up in a loose box away from the hens. The garden looked good as did the ploughed fields, which were now ready for another rotary hoeing prior to planting, first the fruit trees then the berry bushes ready for spring. Next in line were the root crops, peas, and broad beans. They were all going to be very busy once the spring weather arrived. He was mindful of the fact, that all the bee hives needed to be attended to whilst awaiting the sunshine, He needed to move six or so hives up to Skelton Gardens ahead of the spring flowering of the fruit trees.

Back then to Spring Gardens as he decided to name the home property and Spring Farms across the road, being the new name for

Metcalf's farm. The stall was still exceptionally busy but, after all it was Saturday, the busiest day of each week. Everything had apparently travelled well in his absence except for the mail, and other paperwork, which would have to wait until the morrow. Paper work was always a serious problem and unless it was attended to promptly it quickly became a nightmare. There were all sorts of penalties and consequences waiting the unwary, for example it was the easiest thing in the world to lose one's credit rating in the financial world with only one missed payment of account. Although spring was still a long way off, all the hives needed to be checked repaired and refurbished where necessary. The new boxes constantly arriving from the College allowed him to keep the bees comfortably housed with solid frames and boxes. Honey was quickly becoming a main income business, and was valuable enough to justify all the work needed to keep everything in tiptop order. Transporting the hives from site to site really did pay off. Keeping the bees close to the flowers made the returns much more acceptable, and defining the different

305

classifications of the honey meant a solid increase in the price received and rewards for extra effort. His accountant, Alex Littlewood, suggested that it was now time to purchase and fit up a new and possibly bigger van or Pantechnicon with a better overhead gantry before the end of the tax year to get the best results from the system.

Ray began looking through the trade advertisements for suitable vehicles, that he could adapt for his purpose. Much of the research was done by telephone and some dealership visits. Eventually he was left with the decision, new or old. The government was offering substantial rebates on new vehicles, in an attempt to prop up the vehicle manufacturers, and reduce unemployment. This meant that the new vehicle was more beneficial because of the extra depreciation rates each tax year. He decided to hang on to the aging Ford Trader van to act as a back-up to any new one. He would have it thoroughly refitted as a tax deduction. It would fit in as a small run-about and was still suitable for use at Ostaly on sale days. Greg was now operating at Ostaly four days each week and had found it necessary to take one of the younger staff members with him. He took the big trailer most days with back-up stock

So, Ray and Jenifer went for a prowl around the dealer's, yards over the next few weeks. He was offered quite a few deals but was in no real hurry yet. Out of the blue, he received a call from a dealer in Bradford who handled stock from a few different manufacturers. He said he had heard on the grape vine that Raymond was looking for a heavy van of some sort. He offered to call and collect Ray and drive him to his yard where he believed he would find something very suitable. When he arrived at the farm, Ray showed him the Trader van suggesting that a bigger brother of that was what he needed. He pointed out that he had to access some difficult sites so needed it to be compact but strong and powerful. The dealer, Laurie, reckoned he had the very thing just arriving. At the dealership yard Ray was shown a number of big vans but none pleased him. Somewhat disappointed he was about to insist on a ride home when he spotted a large van entering the yard. Laurie with some relief, pointed to it saying, "Ah! ha! Here it is, this is what I was hoping to show you. This lorry was ordered by a furniture removalist who has since gone bankrupt, so I have to find a new buyer for it very quickly and it's a bit of a speciality. I can give you first choice if it suits. I have just had it delivered from Glasgow so it needs an on-road service ready to go to work. It was built on sixteen-inch wheels to keep it nice and low. This is an Albian Terrier. It comes with a five-speed gearbox and two speed rear axle which should get you anywhere you need to go. The power steering is top notch making it easy to manoeuvre, in tight spaces. It comes with a powerful diesel engine., We'll have to have a gantry arrangement built for it of course. Hop in and take it for a drive and get the feel for it. Ray wasn't going to be rushed, until after a circular tour of the roads nearby. He needed to match the lorry up to the gantry designs that he and Mr. Robertson had made out. The next morning, he went to the college to have a chat with his old tutor. After much discussion about the pros and cons they decided that the

Albion would be as near to ideal as possible, especially when fitted with a dual gantry and extending arms. The Albion was fitted with 24 volt electrical system allowing the use of an electric winch to raise the hives. Ray let the matter rest until the following week when Jenifer drove him to the yard. Laurie was glad to see him but cooled a little when Ray offered his ultimatum regarding the price. He showed Laurie working drawings of the gantry and he was taken to a nearby engineering works. The new gantry was expensive as expected, but still well within his budget. The engineering firm was also able to supply two 24 volt electrical winches and wiring to suit. Finally, a deal was agreed to although the dealer wasn't very happy, even though he would receive commission on the sale of the gantry. He insisted on a large holding fee to cover his expenses. Ray paid him and the engineering firm in full. He was told that it would take a week or so to complete ready for delivery. They said that the gantry would only have a maximum load limit of 1ton which suited Ray's requirements anyway.

On the way home Jenifer asked him to pull up somewhere quickly. She scrambled from the car and vomited on the grass verge. Once she settled down again, she stumbled back into the car and Ray asked, "That's not the first time is it sweetheart?"

She looked at him slyly and admitted that he was correct. He drove her straight round to their local doctor who confirmed that she was with child, maybe 7 or 8 weeks in fact. They were both delighted but Ray said, "I suppose you'll use this as an excuse to get out of work. Just when I've managed to get you working without wages, you pull this one on me."

Jenifer said, "You are a rotten pig, Ray Clarke. I'll get you back for that"

"I was only joking love. I don't care whether you do or not. Just look out for yourself and our baby."

Margaret called in at their home when they got back to see if they had bought the lorry. Ray stood up and retorted, "Margaret, your daughter has let me down badly. She has been playing around and gotten herself pregnant. She is with child. Doctor Smythe has just confirmed it. Bang goes my peace and serenity. Now I'll have to cook my own meals and do the laundry as well as the vacuuming."

Margaret took a few minutes to absorb all that nonsense, before wrapping herself around Jenifer and showering her with tears and kisses. Next it was Ray's turn, then she opened up both arms and hugged them all together. It might have gone on all night but Ray stated, "Hey cut that out woman, I desperately need a mug of strong, sweet tea to settle my nerves. I've had a terrible day. I have just spent a fortune on a new lorry and now this on top. How much worse can it get."

Eventually they discovered that the baby was a cute little boy. The mother and baby thrived from day one, and Jenifer took great delight in breast feeding him. Anette was delighted, and nearly wore a groove across the road, due to her many excursions to take her turn at cuddling, changing, then feeding the little blighter. The house was constantly full of admiring women and girls, all taking a turn for cuddles. Even Ray got more than his share as well, both with the baby, and some of the women and girls. This delightful baby boy was the start of an avalanche of humanity, four in all, three boys and one girl. As Ray said, they were always looking out for new staff members so why not breed his own.

Shortly after the new lorry arrived, Alister caught up with Ray. He said, "Ray, I've been taking Shauna out socially and I need to talk about the cottage where I'm living. We were hoping you might be agreeable to us getting married, and living in the cottage. I know it will mean a bit more travelling to get her to work here. It will be easy if we are working together here or there; but some days we'll need to work apart but Shauna can work at Skelton gardens instead of me. She and Elizabeth get on great together and I can work over here doing her jobs."

"I should say that will be excellent. Why did I think you were going to tell me she was expecting? Work out some suitable dates and we can have another party or two. It makes a nice change from funeral wakes. Congratulations and best wishes from me and mine. Here; shake my hand, young man. I suppose her parents approve the match and will be happy if she is living out at Skelton Gardens, with you. It's a fair way to travel, but you have your Norton and dad has a decent car"

"Yes, they are delighted and it gives them more room for the rest of our mob. They will all miss Shauna, but so what. The whole mob of them will probably spend a fair bit of time at weekends and school holidays, messing about among the poultry and maybe helping hand with chores. The three oldest would be able to help with the seasonal work to earn some pocket money as well.

In fact, the older siblings spent most of their weekends out at Skelton. They soon worked out a suitable roster. They walked to the stall after school on Fridays and stayed all weekend, camping with either Gregory, Elizabeth, or Alister, which ever took their fancy, and were dropped off at school on Monday morning."

"Ok then, that's another problem sorted. Let's get some more carrots washed then we can finish up for the day." Shauna had been part of Ray's operation for a long time, firstly as a part timer when still at school, then full time for

313

the last year or so. She was a keen worker and always ready to adapt to new ideas. She could be relied upon to arrive on time and put in the extra mile when needed, even though she had a decent bike ride to get to and from home. When the weather was very bad, Ray loaded her bike in the van and delivered her to her home safely. He was very happy to espouse this union and help with their relationship. Alister's suggestions should work well for all concerned. Maybe she could help out at Mabel's place as well because Mabel was getting bogged down with the honey business and of late her pickles, relishes, chutneys and Jams were selling extra well. Alister could simply drop her off on his way to work and collect her on the way home. Most of the hotels, caterers and restaurants were keen to use more of their products, so they were now using much larger bottles and jars as an extra to the household bottles. As a result, she needed extra staff full time to cope with the output. Ray had found some used catering machinery, that with a little modification, by himself, and the college students, would greatly speed up Mabel's operations and reduce manual labour. Mabel's operation was fast becoming a major part of the business and it reduced much of the otherwise waste vegetables and fruit. Often Alister's family would ride in the side car to spend the whole day at Mabel's place, sterilising, labelling, bottling and generally helping out. They were good little workers and earned the money paid to them but they were tired out by the time Greg collected them in the evening ready for a nice soaking bath before dinner.

Once Alister and Shauna were married it wasn't long before Shauna was with child, much to everyone's delight and the older kids were waiting, somewhat impatiently, I might add, for the big event. Their first-born child was a gorgeous little girl who they named Gwen. The older kids swamped the nursery as did Grandparents and others. Everyone wanted a turn at cuddling and feeding except at 2.00am, when it was left for Shauna to attend to.

With now around one hundred hives in production, Ray and Greg were flat out throughout the warmer months, moving hives to better sites, changing honey frames and delivering them to Mabel. Ray's idea of spare bee boxes and frames was a real winner. It meant a fast turn-around on site and all the honey was extracted in the honey rooms at Mabel's place to assure against any contamination. Mabel now had five different blends of honey and lots of bottled vegetables and pickles which kept her, and her staff busy. They even needed a good deal of help from the main crew at Spring Gardens when the soft fruits were ripe and other orchard fruits like plums were ready for picking and jam making. Pruning was a huge project each Autumn and winter, but there was no hurry with that. Ray invited the college students to visit and learn some of the tricks of the trade, including grafting, and budding and espalier set up. Many of the older varieties of fruits had been regrafted giving them a new lease of life. There was an unexpected bonus in the orchards at Xmas time because many of the older apple trees had been impregnated by mistletoe which was always in short supply. Ray even went so far as to collect as many seeds as possible after Xmas for which he paid the kids pocket money. He printed out notices to display on the stall and other venues asking for donations of used mistletoe berries. These seeds he impregnated onto many of the apple trees under his management, to keep up the supply for future years.

Ray realised that there was a potential problem looming for the future, Mabel had always managed to keep her little bottling factory below the regulations but it had become so busy that, inevitably, the council would start asking awkward questions and close her down. He called in to see her for a chat to overcome the possibility of her being shut down, even for a short period. There was plenty of room at Mabel's place to erect a decent building to house the extraction and bottling plant combined with, or separate, from the vegetable processing plant. He suggested that he could buy her property or lease most of it from her. The alternative would be to build a new plant either at Spring Farm or Spring Gardens. Ray was aware that he would have to now register the operations and comply with the current rules and regulations, re ablution

317

blocks for staff, drainage, and access roads. He would need to licence the factory with permission from council and work within their rules. Cap-in-hand, so to speak, he went for a visit at the council offices and outlined his plans without discussing the present facility.

Mabel owned up to the fact that she was getting a bit long-in-the -tooth for all that, so she agreed to sell the property. A deal was finally engineered allowing Mabel and her entourage to live in the house and run her garden, poultry, pigs, and a goat or two as well as a couple of bee hives.

The council engineers and health officials arranged to visit Spring Farm, and talk through the different options allowing them to move forward with a minimum of disruption. The council agreed to allow the current bottling factory to continue working, pending imminent construction of a new factory on some available land at Spring Farm. Ray was pleased with that arrangement because it brought the operations under one roof so to speak and he was able to let Mabel keep the existing extractor for her own private use. The new factory would be closer to all amenities and road access, as well, as on his home and door step.

All that, meant Raymond was going to be swamped with work again until the new place was ready. Once installed it would save much labour, and greatly speed up each section. With some government help, both financial and physical, he decided to take advantage of the new government assistance package to increase the job advantages for disabled workers. The bottling factory was ideally set up for this type of input, and he arranged machines and conveyers to suit. Toilet and other personal facilities had to be included, but there was financial, and design help to accomplish all that.

The exercise meant a good deal more ongoing paperwork to meet the departments guidelines, however, that was accomplished by engaging a partially disabled lady in the office. He found a very capable and experienced lady, who had become wheel chair dependant due to a motoring accident. The lady, Elizabeth, had good working knowledge with the new computers that seemed to be, "all the go", at that time, and the department provided free training at a nearby college to keep her up to date with the technology. As the college was quite close, Ray allowed the tutors to hold sessions in his offices using his new computers, and learning their use in a real workplace to deal with wages, stock control and many other mundane, and boring tasks with ease. All this input enabled him to keep up with the latest technology as it came on stream, often with little financial costs due to an arrangement with the department and college.

In the new factory, the hives flowed through on a conveyor belt directly off the pallets along one wall, with sufficient storage before and after extraction for the boxes. So too, the vegetables would flow on two conveyors, one for preparation, and one for bottling and labelling. Once the ground work was completed the building quickly became a reality. By leaving the old equipment at Mabel's the new and better machinery was soon installed and working. The waste water was channelled into a large concrete sump from where it could be pumped through a series of irrigation pipes back onto the orchard and garden, to improve the size and quality of the fruit. Many improvements had been incorporated at Mabel's place over time, but there was now room for quite big changes to the trees, and garden area, to maximise production. Furthermore, machinery manufacturers were bursting their boxes to get in on the act, designing new machines and conveyors, using modern techniques and technology.

The E.E.C. inspectors turned up eventually. Ray managed to keep the various properties separate, making them look like small hobby farms rather than one massive outfit. Spring Gardens and Spring farm, however came under severe scrutiny. Spring Farm was treated as an industrial plant, which it was, only the orchard part was suspect, but Ray was able to get around many of the rules and regulations, provided he did not sell any produce through the markets. Because of those and other rulings, Ray, looked around for some way of diverting most of the E.E.C. rulings and accidentally found a solution. The copious amount of out of season production was a big help but more was needed. One of his younger staff members was waiting for his return from Skelton Springs one afternoon. Rosalind had been with him from her twelfth birthday as a part-timer and became full time on her fifteenth birthday. She was a valued and eager worker and he respected her input. When Ray asked her what she was doing still at the farm this late, she said, "Mister Raymond, I am really sorry about this but I really needed to talk with you, because I believe it could mean more business for the firm, and new experiences for me."

"Ok Rosalind, once I get the kettle on, and with a nice brew in hand, you can tell me what's on your mind. I can't make any promises until I know all the details."

She responded, "Yes I realise that. My Grandfather is a keen gardener and he needs some help and encouragement. He grows lots of flowers, many of which are out of season, such as daffodils at Xmas, and others that are somewhat exotic and need extra care. He has a small greenhouse but can't afford heating. He wondered if you have any space, especially after the tomatoes have finished in the autumn, where he could produce seedlings and cuttings and pot plants for you to sell on your stall. Would you have a few moments one day to listen to his ideas and see if any of it would work here."

"Right you are my girl. It's getting late now and you have a fair way to travel, so pop your bike in the Thames van and I'll run you home to meet your Grandfather."

"Wow Mr. Ray, that would be great. I never expected anything as quick as that. Let's go." He helped her load her bike and away, they went. After introductions, her Grandfather, Roger, began to expand some of his ideas. To get started, he pointed to the many varieties of geraniums around his garden, he had a magnificent display of many colours and types. He explained to Ray that as soon as autumn weather closed in and frosts became a reality, he was forced to remove most of the "wood" and top growth and deposit it in the compost heap. Where-as, if he had a heated greenhouse, like Raymond's, he could strip them all out to make cuttings ready for next year. He said he could use up some of the depleted soil, ex-tomatoes, pack it into trays, and root many new geraniums, which he could transplant out in the spring into plastic pots for sale on the stall. He told Ray that the depleted soil could be refurbished with trace elements and fertilisers at very little cost, to replant the new shoots. He wanted to continue along those lines, but Ray had to stop him and get home, with promises to follow up the ideas and get back to him.

After much thought Ray decided to go along with Roger's suggestions but only at Spring Farm initially. Because it was listed as a farm the E.E.C. inspectors targeted it and were always complaining. The flower business did not come within their mandate so he gave Gordon a free hand. Gordon was not looking for a source of income, only something to fill his days, and amuse himself, so it would be mainly profit on the stall, except for pots, and he could drive Rosalind to and from work.

As autumn was upon them, Gordon stripped as much wood as possible from the geraniums, and other suitable varieties of garden plants. Not only his own, but there were many available on Ray's properties as well as others around the area. He had hundreds of cuttings and was going to be busy when transplanting time came along. He also checked out and removed all the strawberry runners that showed promise as well as rehousing his begonia collection. Those he cut back to obtain as many cuttings as possible and now it was up to mother nature to do her stuff. Ray supplied him with a good many spring bulbs and pots, to pot up for Xmas. Fortunately, the new breed of plastic pots, were considerably cheaper than the old terracotta pots, much lighter, easier to stack and sterilise. All the old top soil in the hot houses needed to be dug out and replaced for the next crop anyway, so instead of dumping it in the orchard much of it was carefully stacked in a spare corner of the yard and left to rot and mature ready for reuse on the flowers. Spring and early summer would tell if the idea was a winner.

Once the plants burst into flower, they were grabbed up eagerly, much to Roger's delight. He had been worried sick in case the plants did not sell well, and he was greatly relieved.

Rosalind helped him as much as possible between her other work, especially on her days off. Both of them were avid flower growers. They began studying books and catalogues for more ideas and inspiration. Some plants would need much more careful attention to the growing medium to suit their roots, like members of the orchid family, which were only parasites needing very open potting mix, which was very free draining. They needed very little moisture at all, they were designed to flourish on the bark of tropical trees, with no soil around them, as does mistletoe on apple trees. Roger was eager to experiment with temperature and humidity levels, there were some failures, alongside many successes. He pointed out that he had no other interests so he concentrated on his flowers seven days each week, with Rosalind's help of course. Rosalind was relieved of most of her usual work to enable her to work full time with Gordon when, required.

Even Ray's hotel customers were beginning to get excited, needing flower arrangements and potted plants throughout their premises.

Ray began planting flowers among other crops for the cut flower trade. With Roger's and Rosalind's input to design suitable plots for viewing as well as harvesting, he planted spring bulbs throughout the orchards and around the fruit trees, which produced a vast amount of saleable blooms when the orchards were otherwise dormant. Substantial beds of daffodils, tulips and many other spring bulbs, were soon producing extra income and employment for the casual labour force in the off season. Some flower plants such as marigolds were a valuable addition to the garden, helping with pest and fungus control. Because he could market all this produce direct to existing customers, and any new businesses, there was a decent profit to be made and little or no waste. The main expense was the purchase of huge amounts of assorted pots and decorative containers, and this as well as other reasons caused him to purchase a second-hand forklift and a stack of pallets to go with it. The spring bulbs were soon producing cut flowers for sale and Roger hunted around his friends to obtain root stock of chrysanthemums, and dahlia tubers. Carnations were sown from seed and many recovered from old root stock. He scoured the countryside and markets to obtain sufficient root stock to add to annual seedlings. Also, he planted out many species that yielded foliage only, such as maiden-hair ferns, to round out the displays. Many seedlings he planted in small tubs for sale and home planting. These were eagerly taken by the customers and even council gardens and hotels.

The flowers and garden plants business eased the pressure put on by the E.E.C. and added another successful branch to Ray's business empire. The final results came home when a couple of flower shops, and even nurseries began to exploit Gordons stock of young plants. Spring happened suddenly that year and a great many plants were needed urgently. Having the heated greenhouses gave Ray a good start to the season, so he could fill commercial orders before the opposition got started. He had a huge stock of well rooted geraniums and pelargoniums ready for transplanting and the councils took most of them. Roger hurried around to find Ray and tell him about the council deal, and requested assistance, to load and transport them onto sites around the city, where they were needed. The hot house was now almost empty so planting could begin for summer vegetables like cucumbers and some tomatoes and the old bloke was quite ecstatic.

The sudden activity by the council, and to a lesser extent the hotels, was soon producing a big problem due to an accumulation of used pots and containers. Ray realised that he could capitalise on this problem because he had plenty of steam and hot water from his boilers enabling him to sterilise and recycle, not only his own pots, but many more from other sources. He was soon selling pots, especially the decorative ones, and using the cheap ones himself. The world appeared to be almost perfect for a few months until Ray received a great shock that was to set him on his backside for months. Everything had to stop around Spring Farm and Spring Gardens. There was no room for any further development and it appeared that he might lose a good deal of his current holdings, if not all of them, with catastrophic consequences.

As the day was settling in one Monday morning a couple of surveyors turned up at Spring Gardens and began to set up their equipment. Ray walked over and demanded an explanation. The surveyors told him that they were working on an extension from the A1{M} motorway to pick up the major access roads further south feeding Wakefield, Huddersfield, Oldham, Manchester Nottingham city, Leicester City. The preliminary survey, mainly aerial photographs, showed it would run right through his property and all three houses and all his buildings would have to be forfeited to allow that to happen. Ray went berserk. After a long argument, which ended in him evicting the surveyors from his property, he made an appointment with his solicitor, Mr. Wilkinson The surveyors worked either side of Spring Gardens, and assured him that a compulsory purchase order would take it from him anyway. Ray went into his office and called Mr Wilkinson, his solicitor. His solicitor said that if the land was needed for road works there was very little he could do to stop it, but if he challenged it strongly he might delay the inevitable for a year or two. He suggested that Ray speak to an Estate Valuer and obtain an accurate valuation of the said properties. He thought that if the valuation proved to be very high which he was certain it would be, they may divert the bye-pass around to the East of his property. Ray organised a valuation, and a specialist valuer called around the following week. Apart from all the buildings, and other infrastructure such as the green houses, he had to allow for the value of the business and all the improvements, growing crops, and many other assets, such as the mushroom cellars and poultry houses.

He had all sorts of maps and plans and suggested alternative routes, none of which would help much. The valuer was in some doubt about the logistics of even challenging the county road authority, then he suddenly came upon an idea that might work in Ray's favour. Turning to Ray he asked, "I don't suppose you've had any visits from the heritage society in recent months. They're travelling around the area and listing old buildings with possible heritage value. This main house is very old by the look of it, as are the farm buildings. Do you happen to know when they were built, and did they include it in their survey?"

Ray told him that the heritage people had given him a hard time, insisting that the properties would be listed with all sorts of strict conditions about their future use and development. He said, "Hang on a moment, I'll just get the papers that the heritage people left me. They are determined that the whole property, including both houses and all the barns are to be Grade 2 heritage listed. Also, Spring Farm across the road, and from now on I'll need to get permission for any alterations or modifications. They took a series of photographs from all angles to log onto the file, and everything will need to comply with those photographs. Not only the external walls but much of the interior has to remain as is for ever. Even the farm land surrounding my property will be included."

"Do you know who owns the grazing land around your place?"

"Yes, of course. I know all about that farm. I own all of the 350 acres here, and 375 acres over the road, although some is leased to a neighbouring dairy farmer." Ray said.

"Well no matter that it's leased. you own the title. They will have to move the road further out of your area. They cannot interfere with heritage property without a great deal of rigmarole, so it is my guess they will start again and realign the road further out"

"Not too much further out because I own two more properties out in that direction but there should be plenty of room for them in between. I just hope they make cross over roads or under-passes so we can gain access to all my properties without too much extra travelling."

That was the beginning of months of haggling and negotiations, mainly between the heritage people, the county council and department of main roads, with some input by Ray and his solicitor. However, the matter was eventually put to rest, with the formal approval of new plans to site the road further East, creating a significant, southwards bump in the new motorway, and clear of all Ray's property, much to his relief. Surprisingly only a week after receiving the news, a representative of the main roads department, the chief engineer to be exact, called at Spring Gardens and introduced himself. Over a pot of coffee and snacks, the engineer apologised for all the trouble and expense that he had created, explaining that he only studied the topography of the area with the aid of the aerial photographs to select the best route for the new road. It was only when the flack finally reached his desk, he realised that an alternative route had to be found. He was delighted with what he saw at Spring Gardens and Spring Farm. He pointed out that many buildings of similar age were in poor or even dilapidated condition, and he congratulated Raymond on the condition of his buildings, which would last for many years to come. Finally, he said, "All these problems must have cost you a good deal of money. You must have a decent bill from your solicitor and the surveyors, which you can submit direct for my personal attention, and I'll send you a compensation cheque to cover most of that expense." So, saying, he shook hands with Ray, and departed with a box of fruit and vegetables for his trouble. He pointed out that he and his family lived out Shipley way and he would bring his wife over to the stall on a weekend shopping trip or two in the future. Raymond was fortunate to have completed most of the changes and alterations to his properties prior to the heritage people arriving and the bottling factory became an integral part of the heritage. All the external building work such as the factory walls and vegetable stand had been camouflaged to blend in with the heritage features. Many of the vertical sections had been covered with espalier lattice and were now growing with soft fruits and fruit trees,

With the road problem sorted, Ray settled down to a more organised life with Jenifer and the kids, four at that moment in time, three robust boys and a delightful little girl at the end of the run. Keeping tabs on income tax was an ongoing problem but his accountant, Alex Littlewood, was a genius in sorting out ways and means to minimise the pain. Employing a number of invalid workers proved to be a benefit rather than an expense, and Ray's office manager, Elizabeth, seemed to have a handle on all the requirements needed to keep the authorities happy. She alone managed to sort out the wages and adjustments as well as organising the paperwork to gain maximum amounts of compensation for each disabled employee. She was required to categorise each worker according to their disabilities and select new employees with the required abilities from time to time to best fill vacancies as they occurred. She kept a list of details of would be applicants, to assess their individual skills and abilities with the view to slotting them into the workforce when needed. Ray and his friends at the college were needed to rearrange and redesign new situations, or adjust and modify existing work stations to fit potential applicants.

Overall, one of his biggest concerns was dealing with the various authorities who it seemed were only trying to create more work for their own departments. What with various, so called experts, from the council, the government, and the E.E.C. he was always busy wasting time and resources that would have been better spent in other ways. They were forever turning up unannounced, trying to find unnecessary additions to the infrastructure to fulfil their own ideas.

Each inspector had his own interpretation of the rule book, just like Christians reading the bible, each sect and denomination read the same book but interpreted it differently to suit their own ideas. The worst of these experts were the inspectors from the newly created Health and Welfare departments and the fire brigade. After their initial visits and inspections Ray upgraded his facilities to comply with the regulations as specified. The next time someone called, and it was seldom the same people, they had different interpretations of the regulations and needed everything changed to suit. The fire brigade were the worst. They claimed that he had installed the wrong type of extinguishers in all the wrong positions. The fire extinguisher problem soon came to a brick wall when the latest so called, expert, arrive to inspect the factory and other areas. He was a bouncing, bumptious, know-all, who was determined to make a name for himself, and cover himself with glory. He pointed out, once again, that Raymond had purchased the wrong type of extinguishers including the wrong makes, as well as wrong sizes, and installed them in all the wrong positions. Ray had bought Simplex extinguishers as per instructions from previous representatives and installed them as described, but the new chappie was not happy. Ray asked him to make out a list of the correct appliances and using chalk make out and number each site and the appropriate location. This done Ray smelled a rat. He had not only named the appropriate appliances but listed Langdon and Saroson catalogue numbers as well. According to him all the other appliances were to be disposed of immediately.

Ray realised that the new representative had some sort of alliance with the company, Langdon and Saroson and was probably receiving commissions for each new sale. He asked the representative if he would be good enough to wait over a mug of tea or coffee whilst he made an urgent phone call or two. Reading off the new paperwork he called the department offices and asked for the area manager. After some delay a polite sounding gent who claimed he was the area manager, asked him, what was the reason for the call. Without delay, Ray weighed in with a question, asking, "Excuse me Sir, are you also reaping rewards and commissions from Langdon and Saroson, for the sale of their fire extinguishers, as is your agent."

The area manager replied indignantly, "No I damned well aren't. What the hell is all this about? Are you questioning my honesty and dedication to this department? Please explain yourself immediately and it had better be good, or else I'll sue the pants off you. How dare you suggest any such thing?" Quite calmly, Ray explained what had just happened, much to the dismay of the area manager, who asked if the representative was still at the farm. Ray reported that, indeed the chappie was still in his outer office. And, yes, he would allow him to speak to his boss on the telephone. After a serious verbal spat, the area manager terminated the employment of his representative, and called him back to his office immediately, to return the department's car and files. The representative was, of course, furious with Ray and threatened retribution, as he stormed out of the office and drove away. A few days later Ray received a letter of apology, and a note of thanks, for jumping in and averting more possibilities of further incidents of that kind. The letter also stated that the firm in question had been severely spoken to. The manager of the supply firm, was just as astounded as the area manager, and had fired their sales Representative on the spot. Obviously, a serious lecture was needed to educate all reps on correct protocol in future. All this was uncalled for and created much unnecessary expense, and wasted time in his already busy life.

All this nonsense aside, most officials of one sort or another were very cooperative and assisted wherever possible. The local town and shire engineers especially, along with their staff of competent and loyal workers, often stepped in, to smooth out some of the rough patches. Many of these local officers were regular patrons of the roadside shop, and wanted it to continue to thrive. Also, Ray was employing some of their family members in his business, often part-time from their twelfth birthdays and throughout their teenage years, adding valuable income to struggling low income families.

Looking back over the years, Raymond was astounded that he had progressed from being orphaned to ending up with his own "empire" employing many workers, especially the numerous invalid and disabled people. Occasionally he sat down to discuss their situation with Elizabeth in the office, checking overall staff numbers, and percentages of disabled personnel. It was Elizabeth who pointed out to Ray that the number of their disabled workers, needed to be multiplied by the number who had successfully gained sufficient confidence in their own limited abilities, to move out from under their care and settle down to work in other industries, and even excel in the general community. They often had potential employers calling in and discussing various staff members, with a view to employing them or someone with similar disabilities. The compensation being paid by the various government departments, made it lucrative to add disabled personnel to their workforce, and often the rewards were unexpectedly greater, due to their greater output from being able to focus exclusively on one aspect of the job. Another advantage of employing a number of disabled people was a surprise. These people have often excelled in their endeavours, then gone out into the workplace and society in general, and were able to sell their results to other similarly handicapped people and get them out to work, at least partially, and sometimes completely independent. Ray, and others around him, were astounded with the difference the ability to work and gain acceptance, lifted these people to a new level of self-esteem. It's hard to explain to others what this means to such people until you witness it for yourself. Not all the disabled, but certainly a good percentage of them, moved forward into a new and exciting world. Many of them have been disadvantaged from birth, or an early age, and become used to existing that way and they show the most improvement. A new world awaits them, whereas others, have often lived a "normal" life until disablement was thrust upon them due to accident or illness.

Ray accepted this unexpected glory, and was, therefore, able to help others and move on to greater heights. In spite of all his business successes, Ray's greatest pleasures came from his bee keeping work. He so enjoyed working with the bees that he was doing most of the hive work leaving the honey business to Mabel and her crew. Ray took great pleasure in lying in the heather watching the bees at work. Their energy was continuous, never ceasing from early day-light to dusk, whenever the weather allowed them to work. Bees do not like to get wet and so seemed to know when to leave the hive and when not to, He learned that they had special dances which they performed on the honey comb to tell their fellow bees what sort of blossoms were available and which direction to travel to locate them. They even had a special code to let the others know how far away certain flowers could be found, thus saving much energy searching.

Whilst working within the hives, it quickly became apparent that the bees had a special arrangement among their kind, to work out which bees worked at which tasks, each day. The breeding cycle was carefully organised, to make sure that only one queen could attend to the breeding, and no others could interfere. Each queen laid eggs almost continuously, producing millions of replacement young bees to keep the hive in full production.

Sometimes a young female would unite with a drone causing them to be expelled from the hive to find a suitable home for a new swarm, If this expulsion was late in the autumn, the young couple would have little time to find a new home before the bad weather settled in and they would perish. To these ends and to prevent this loss Ray often set up a new box and combs close to each group of hives and thus produce a new colony and increase his flow of honey. Sometimes the new swarm was not well organised and the hive failed, but many of them did thanks in part to the diligence of the local college handicraft section, who manufactured a continuous supply of boxes and frames to fit them. Ray started with Forty working hives, and over the following couple of summers ended up with around one hundred. It was a big undertaking to move them around from crop to crop, to obtain the maximum amount of honey each season, and swap all the frames as they became full.'

Ray was leading an exciting life full of surprises each day. It had been tough in the early days but now he was quite fulfilled with a lovely young family and many friends around him and a good steady income.

POST SCRIPT

Orphaned at the tender age of twelve, Raymond was left without house, home, and family due to a serious road accident, which killed his parents and sister. With only his disabled Grandmother for support, he was forced to move out of house and home immediately, and clear all his family possessions. He had some help from a family friend, and members of the Roman Catholic convent in Clifford village, to organise the funerals of his family, as well as find a new home and college.

Whilst attempting to load his family possessions, his father's boss, who always claimed to be a Christian gentleman, physically assaulted him, after trying to steal the family pigs. Raymond retaliated and won the day. He had to move into his Grandmother's little council cottage, and it was there that, he spotted an advertisement about a college near Leeds, who had vacancies for new students for the coming year.

The inquiry about the college led him to new beginnings and a new life.

346

By working very hard, physically and mentally, both at college and at home, he was able to turn these small beginnings into a successful life, for himself and his Grandmother. On the way, Raymond lost his aging Grandmother, his patron, and his elderly neighbours due to old age and infirmity Now alone in the world again, Raymond was able to turn many of these disadvantages to profit at each opportunity, and build up a satisfactory life for himself.

Love and romance gave him a kick in the teeth. Just another adversity to overcome whilst his business kept him too busy to worry. He had a number of invalid employees to look after by then, and lots of aggro from various government departments.